William Stephens Hayward

The Colonel's Daughter

A Romance

William Stephens Hayward

The Colonel's Daughter
A Romance

ISBN/EAN: 9783337348830

Printed in Europe, USA, Canada, Australia, Japan

Cover: Foto ©Andreas Hilbeck / pixelio.de

More available books at **www.hansebooks.com**

THE
COLONEL'S DAUGHTER.

A Romance.

By W. S. HAYWARD,

AUTHOR OF "HUNTED TO DEATH," "LOVE AGAINST
THE WORLD," &C., &C.

LONDON
JOHN AND ROBERT MAXWELL
MILTON HOUSE, 4, SHOE LANE FLEET STREET.

CONTENTS.

iv   CONTENTS.

THE COLONEL'S DAUGHTER.

CHAPTER I.

A HAMERTON HEROINE BEFORE THE LETTERS.

WHEN you are flying over hill and down to Brighton from the metropolis, by the aid of that magnified iron fly of Regiomantus which we call the railway engine, you must often have seen one especially bewitching patch of landscape, rivulet, mead, wood, grazing lambs and colts, meditative cows, all the features of a cabinet picture. You gaze spellbound, and long to be housed in one of those villas which flash back the sun from windows on high through cordons of trees. But suddenly your envy is dispelled; you perceive, like a baleful shadow on an enormous sundial, a factory chimney projecting rigid, smooth, inartistic, from a square box of brick: it is a factory. Arcadia vanishes, and you think of the Black Country.

If you could only ignore that detestable column, with its perpetual oozing forth of dun-coloured smoke, and the hideous screech of its "siren" steam whistle, you would love to linger in that scenery.

On the watercourse which glutted the factory boiler, but at some distance from the works, a young man and a girl were idly floating in a light pleasure-boat. The reeds, cress and rushes formed a screen where they were embayed, and they were watching the tiny clouds on the verge of the horizon. Violet, grey, and silvery, with a fringe of pure white on their upper edges, like so much sea foam. Thence uprose the sky in a clear deep blue, glorious, but about to fade before the stars, a signal that daylight has departed. In the zenith were hovering two or three clouds more solid and quite motionless. A vast sheet of light was spreading over the shallow waters, sleeping in one spot, sparkling in another, where the fish swarmed and leaped for midges, making argentine wavelets tremble in the shadows cast by the boat, gilding its sailless mast and lighting up the orange-peel dotting the surface where it had been lately flung. There was a mingling of the features of the country and of urban outskirts on either bank. Rows of pollard willows intervened between houses wide apart, as you find them on first approaching a manufacturing town in a fenny district. There were low-roofed cottages and boarded enclosures, rose gardens (for the standard rose is common at Gratchley), unpainted shutters, workmen's houses, rough and squat ; old, lop-sided arbours for cattle-screens; bits of wall, fresh lime-washed with a whiteness which dazzled with its glare. Then appeared afar dull rows of brick buildings, with red-tiled or dull zinc roofs. From the nearer factory-chimneys ever ascended the columns of smoke, casting a tremulous shadow even across the water. On a board disfiguring the green bank was written, "Hot water for parties;" and before a heap of ruins a larger sign, sunk at one end by its post, bearing "Boats to let;" reminiscences of the days when wayzgoose stewards selected this spot. Over a canal leading to the factory a swing-bridge projected its signal-post, whereunder an angler was leisurely casting and pulling up his regulation two lines. Wheels were faintly creaking, carts rumbling to and fro. Tow-ropes dragged over the hard, black road of cinders, stained with every colour from coal-black to the prismatic hues of oxides, mineral refuse and chemical deposits. From the works low down stole at intervals, on a stratum of air reserved to it alone, an indefinable odour of grease and saccharine clamminess, mixing with the effluvia from standing water in pools, and over-powering the wholesome smell of tar. The silence of the river, where our acquaintances lingered, was continuously disturbed by the beating of trip-hammers and resonant respirations of the powerful engines. It was London, as it were, sending out a picket and planting seeds of Lam-

beth, Rotherhithe and Hoxton, in the depths of
rusticity; one of those jumbles of contrasts
which the etcher delights in, as filthy in parts
as splendid in points; glittering and intensely
shadowed; vulgar, yet not devoid of even Wat-
teau graces; serene, and yet full of life; where
nature cropped up here and there invariably in the
thick of scientific labour and sordid industry, like
a shark's fin cleaving the air on the water's edge
in a remote mouth of a harbour.

"Is it not beautiful?" sighed the girl. "Oh,
wake up, do, please, Mr. Rendall."

"To tell the truth, Miss Pleasanton, I don't feel
the least enthusiasm; though it is beautiful—after
a fashion."

"But it is! I assure you it is. There was
something of this kind at the United Arts Gallery
a couple of years ago, by an Italian who came to
London to paint us at home. No, I don't recollect
his name. I cannot recollect anything just now.
I feel many things which I cannot express."

"True. You are a born artist, Miss Pleasanton."

"Pooh! born fiddlestick," exclaimed she.

"Ha, ha, ha!" laughed he in advance of his
own joke. "It's a pity you are not a born fiddlestick—you might extract more music from your
beau! Like me, his chemist-adviser, your papa's
circle includes only scientific dolts, capitalists and
wholesale druggists,—a most unmelodious throng.
How can you go on loving art, Miss Pleasanton,

in such a ring? Is it they that have disgusted
you with social life? if so, you are wrong: they
are not society. Heaven forbid!"

"Nay, I have seen finer specimens than our
visitors; but I am not interested in them. The
reason, perhaps is, that I have not been very
fortunate in my set. My lot has been cast
among young people of a serious turn, friends of
my brother, *exemplary* young men I assure you,
who would not dream of entertaining young
ladies with any conversation but their last sermon,
the last cantata they were getting up, or the
latest thing in *chasubles*. It is edifying, but I
am not going to be a nun, and the jargon becomes
doleful and monotonous."

"Yes, I know," said Mr. Kendall, with a
smile. "I took one of them, Cubbington, to the
Aquarium, into the Balloon Society's lecture, but,
leaving that room, the Javanese Gamelan players
were on the stage, and I got him to look and
listen. Then he remarked about the female
dancers and the gongs: 'Sort of chimes, eh, eh!
I suppose they are Corean converts, eh, eh? I
heard at Willis's that the Bishop of Ceylon was
prevailing on a party to come over and bear
witness.' But I forgot, you would not know the
town doings. You live under real trees all the
year round."

"Yes, but we are near London: the new service
is rapid. Is that pretty opera at the Comedy

nice ? and the nice comedy at the Opera Comique
pretty ?—how that confuses one ! "

" Oh yes ! the language in one, spoken by Miss
Dollfus, is melodious, and the music in the other
precise as a philologist's. What more can one
desire ? All London goes to both."

" Now only fancy ! the Haymarket is the only
theatre to which I was taken, and that to see Mr.
Buckstone ; and lo ! it was quite a new house,
papa said, and Mr. Buckstone had been out of
the bills for some years ; that shows how little
papa studied the theatrical news. I do not
recall the piece, and, in fact, the audience were
quite a nuisance with bobbing up and down
and craning their necks to one side, because the
Prince and Princess of Wales were in the
royal box. Just as we came in, a foreign woman
in a gorgeous gown with an old-fashioned long
train, was calling out that some one should be
'lashed' or hung on a ' larch ;' but I could not
catch the speech, for she slammed—positively
slammed the door on a gentleman quite violently."

" Yes ; ' Odette,' " said Mr. Rendall, smiling to
himself, " your foreigner is a countess."

" Really, or in the play ? In either case it was
wretched manners. I am fond of plays, though, if
I do not see them."

" That may be the reason."

This young man, who was so prone to dart out
sardonic sallies, was the son of a social wastrel,

whom Colonel Pleasanton had met in Italy, fighting, however, under the French colours. Long
after, the son had come to him with excellent
guarantees of his study in Germany and practical
experience of a varied nature, and the Colonel's
house had become the lonely professor's first
home.

Mrs. Pleasanton had concluded there was no
harm in a gentleman devoted to study, and who
checked the wild rhapsodies of her daughter by
the first non-acquiescence she had ever encountered.

"1 have read several plays, however, and I have
spent some time, I can tell you, in learning 'The
Merry War,' by heart. *You* can go everywhere,
you men; what enviable mortals you must be!
My sister and brother-in-law had an argument the
other evening about the new Almack's. Is it true
that it is risky for a young lady to go there?"

"Impossible! Severity to assert that, Miss Pleasanton! Why not, if you can get a ticket? But
there are places, without being squeamish, where
—hem! if you had said the Criterion."

"Well, the Criterion as a criterion, Mr. Rendall. If you were a married man, would you take
your wife there, even only once, just to see an
act?"

"If I were married, I wouldn't take even
ny—"

"Your mother-in-law, you were going to say.

What a dear ever-living Joe Miller she is! Is it really such a shocking place?"

"*Honni soit.* To such as your surroundings its stalls are the pit of Tophet. Now and then a Frenchy phrase makes *blasé* men lift one or both eyebrows, and women of the world freeze up solid."

"Oh, even in the reserve at Goodwood, I am told, very dreadful language does float to the ear. I should like to see an exciting Derby. It is miserable to be a girl!"

"Not a bit of it! Worshipped, feasted, waited on, hand and foot, or, rather, by horse and foot. Dear Miss Pleasanton, I believe, on the contrary—"

"I only wish *you* were one, sir. You'd soon see how irksome it is to be in a moral strait waistcoat. I know by the eyes of the male wall-flowers that they think when we flourish our fans and keep our eyelashes and lips moving as we confront our partners between the lines on the card, that we are chatting so merrily! I tell you that we are bound to shine in monosyllables; a sort of human revolving light that flashes out 'No, yes,' 'Yes, no,' at intervals. That is the proper thing. I daresay you have been all over the world"— Mr. Kendall nodded pretty comprehensively for so young a man—"and have seen the lasso-men watching a herd of cattle, and when some adventurous animal dares to scamper out of the charmed circle, the leather rope whizzes, catches him in the horrid loop, and he is ignominiously—"

" Yerked, they say."

" How expressive! ' Yerked' back into the mass again; his wishes for fresh fields and pastures new effectually quelled. Mothers always have the social lasso in readiness to *yerk* us back. Even in accomplishments, notability is snubbed. Anything novel in music is a sin, anything grand in drawing is a crime, I do believe. Because I will etch and paint in oils, that annoys the family. I ought to paint nothing but a robin's egg beside a greengage in a toy-basket, in water-colours, and play nothing grander than Schumann. But I am going to destroy the gloomy impression of my character which I have been trying to give you, Mr. Rendall, by confessing that I am getting positively hungry. Shall we catch some fish, and fry them in a gipsy fire on the bank? I should relish that."

" I am afraid," said Rendall, prying alongside, " that frogs are the only edible that abound here. Your father's factory is ' death on fish,' as the Americans would appropriately say. You shudder. You are not equal to frog's legs, I see. I am; for I confess now, Miss Pleasanton, I could do justice to my dinner."

" Ah, I give you notice that I am one of the exceptional women who do eat—even devour."

"Indeed! How, Mademoiselle l'Ogresse!"

"Yes, all my poetry flits from me at meal times. I should be deceiving you if I did not own that I have an appetite. Do you belong to the same clubs, with good *chefs*, as my brother-in-law?"

"Yes, Miss Pleasanton! I belong to the same clubs as Mr. Price. The 'Etheredge,' that's medical; the 'Y Grec,' that's linguistique; the 'Cœur-de-Lion,' that's anythingarian — the— "

"To interrupt you: are there many married men in the 'Cœur-de-Lion?'"

"Yes, very many; rather!"

"That is strange. I cannot understand how a man can leave his sworn companion to amuse himself nightly with boon comrades! Why do you men marry then?"

Mr. Rendall made a face like a Gothic sculptor's gargoyle.

"If I had been a man, I scarcely think I should ever have contemplated marriage," said the girl.

"Well, if people contemplated it, they would hardly plunge. But, fortunately, you are a woman, Miss Pleasanton."

"Yes, yes; woe's me; that is another of our misfortunes : women must not dwell single. But will you tell me why a man joins a club when he gets married? 'When wedlock comes in at the door, love flies out into the club-house window.'"

"Why, in the first place, Miss Pleasanton, every gentleman has to belong to a club—if it were only to let the unlucky know where they are certain to find a lender of assistance at a more or less certain hour! London is so large—think of a fellow who has a hundred pounds to pay, racing all the West End over without some general rendezvous! Heart-breaking! Besides"—here he lit a cigarette before he began to ply the oars, while the girl drew the tiller-lines taut for manipulation—"there's no fear of poisoning yourself alone with your smoker. Do you find any of your neighbours worth visiting?"

"Very, very few! We sometimes go over to Saltwaste to see the Milwards."

"Ah! Milward! I meet him. But is there no one just here to consort with, may I ask?"

"Stay, we have the curate of St. Servanius. Ha, ha! The first time he dined with us, he was so confused that he kept filling all his wine glasses with water, spite of the servant. But I ought to have my tongue slit to tell tales. He is quite a good man, and always bringing me bouquets."

"*Floreat Eto*—is an Eton man, that bashfulness to the contrary? What are the roads like, Miss Pleasanton? Riding must be your principal amusement."

"Yes, I am a Trojan to adore a horse. It is my greatest pleasure, and I do not think I could live without it. But I delight in hunting above all things ; I have been brought up to it in papa's part of the country. Oh, I'm at home on a good horse! Do you know, I have been for seven hours together in the saddle ! "

"Oh, I know all about that ! I learnt in Mexico, when I was silver mining in Sonora. That is centaur-like; no rise and fall on the leather, but holding and guiding the horse between the knees, feeling his every thrill and heart pulsation ; man and animal one, as the Aztecs saw Cortez's chivalry ! Unhappily," added Mr. Rendall, with a smile, as he felt he must damp his listener's enthusiasm, "it makes a man bred to it bow-legged, and all the poetry of the *vaquero* vanishes when you see him waddle along—a mere earthly cowboy."

"But how I like the breeze in one's hair; the music of the hounds, the stirring of the horns, the trees flying before one's eyes! What intoxication ! In such moments I feel as brave as Diana the huntress ! "

"Only at such times, Miss Pleasanton ? "

"I avow it : only then, only when on horseback; for on foot I must tell you I am a great coward, greatly so at night. I don't like thunder, for one thing, at all ; and I am very delighted indeed that those friends have refused our invitation to dinner this evening."

"Why so ? disagreeable? "

" Not they ! but there would have been thirteen
of us—fateful number ! I should have pined for a
lasso to—what is the word?—*yerk* in a fourteenth !
Oh ! there's my brother with the manager, hailing
the boat." They landed. " How beautiful everything looks from this spot!" she continued, pausing
to admire the sunset, "ever beautiful at this hour.'

Evening was closing in. The sky gradually
became tinged with rose colour. A gentle breeze
disturbed the river's surface. The topmost leaves
of the trees trembled, and a paper pin-wheel
began to revolve where some crow-scarer had left
it stuck in the brambles like some new kind of
rose. Two men in tweed suits approached the
young lady and her amateur wherryman, as she
gazed on the sky, and he fastened the boat to
a post before a rude landing-stage. And one of
them, the younger, said in a voice too unctuous to
be vexing, even when raised in irritation :

" What a time you have been on the marsh-
lands, Marsie ! we thought you were devoured by
gnats ! And what does Mr. Rendall," he proceeded in a very soft cooing tone—" what do you
think of our watercourse ? "

" I enjoyed the little cruise under such en-
lightening pilotage very much indeed," evasively
responded the new chemical adviser of the
Gratchley Works.

CHAPTER II.

FRANCIS PLEASANTON was born in the period of the collisions of colossi, the year being 1814, and was the son of an esteemed solicitor and land agent, in Lincolnshire. He entered the army at an early age, but was only an ensign by some strange freak of fortune, up to the overcoming of Scinde. He came out of the Sikh war as a senior lieutenant, with a reputation for invincible courage. In an action in the Punjaub, when, wounded and surrounded by a mass of cavalry in Circassian chain-mail and damascened plate-armour, he was summoned to surrender, he replied by ordering a charge to his handful of horse, and he killed with his own hand three of the stoutest foes. Thus, he cut his way through, followed by his men, but at length having received two bullets in the head, he fell weltering in his blood, and was left for dead. He was a long while recovering, but figured as a captain in the Chinese War, where the accusation fell upon him that he had imitated the French in looting the Palace of Pekin. Offended, he carried his sword to South America, and in

1852 was a colonel in the Brazilian Army, and a special favourite. At the peace he imitated his brothers-in-arms, who, with the extraordinary versatility of Brother Jonathan, laid down sabre and sword for pen and book, and " cramming " rapidly, passed examination to practice as surgeon and physician. His friends at home, more or less influenced (said the slanderous) by the rich and rare (!) Chinese oddities he had presented them some time before, made it smooth at the Horse Guards, and he returned to be shelved according to routine on half-pay. Thus he came home to the old family mansion out of Lincoln, where his mother lived. She was a worthy old dame, such as our age still produces in the provinces, having a merry word for every one, and a preference for wholesome home-brewed to all your light foreign wines. Her son adored her. He found her suffering from an illness of such a nature that medical men had forbidden every kind of stimulant ; he himself gave up wine, spirits, and coffee in order that no temptation might be placed in her way, and to lighten her privation by sharing it with her. He also married to oblige her, out of pious respect for the invalid's wishes. Without overweening inclination for the young lady, he espoused a relation chosen by his mother for those various reasons which unite and interlace families and fortunes in rural districts—an insatiable desire to throw two adjoining estates into one, and so on.

After his mother's death, Colonel Pleasanton having no further inducement to remain in Lincolnshire, and desiring a little to reside in town, sold the house and the rest of his property in the country, except a farm at Seorf-court, and went with his young wife to live on a large estate at Rugemound, in Dorset. Here he owned some ruins of an abbey, a piece of land worthy of the name the monks had given it—Mortomundane, wild and sere, with a large pond and an oak-forest, meadows intersected by stone-walled cuttings, where the clear water ran embowered in foliage, the vegetation of a desert abandoned to itself since 1848, springs in the shade of trees, wild flowers in rank profusion, tracks of semi-wild cattle, ruins of an Italian garden in the midst of decaying buildings. Here and there some traces of the monastic edifice was still standing. The door, and the benches where bread was given to the poor, remained before the entrance porch, tolerably uninjured. Here the battered swordsman fixed his abode.

Here, indeed, he lived till 1837, solitary, buried in study, begun with some view of a public defence of his conduct in the Chinese War, but the attraction of a library led him far afield, till he acquired an extensive range of information, filling his mind, and thoroughly enabling him to master all the industrial sciences. He laid down his books only to take an airing, and to refresh his brain by wearying the body (that mad notion which has its eminent martyrs) in walks of many miles over fields or through the woods. It was a common thing to meet him thus exercising. The labourers recognised him from a great distance, by his long frock-coat, buttoned to the Adam's apple, his long legs of the cavalrist—"the grand limbs of the red devils," which appalled the Chinese, and at which only that dauntless imp, the Parisian caricaturist, dares to poke his crayon —his head somewhat hanging forward, and something like a sword, if only a newly-plucked switch, always in the nervous right hand.

From this retired and laborious life, Colonel Pleasanton only emerged at election times. Then he made his appearance everywhere throughout the neighbourhood. He drove about in a chaise, to kindle with martial fire the passions of the voters when he addressed their meetings. He headed the charge against the Red Tape Department, which he accused of wronging himself (who might have been an U.S.A. general) and innumerable comrades, always easily convincing himself that reform must come with a change of officers, and ignoring the fact that the rank and file of barnacles never are detached from the foundation-rock of the State. Hopefully each time he would none the less be as he returned to the same obscurity to await Justice wielding the glaive.

During this calm, furrowed merely by these

drivings of the political share, two children were born to him ; a boy in 1853, and a girl in the subsequent year. He returned from America in 1863 with an increment of fortune, and he was elected to Parliament. He entered the House full of Transatlantic theories, but, nevertheless, his lively, vigorous, manly and martial language, always full of "strong-horse sense," created a sensation, was heard distinctly by the reporters, and read well in print. He became one of the nightmares of the regular politician and the governing families, for no one could divine what the grey colonel would say next. He was among the grown men what a fiery child is among purist papas and precise mammas, a terror for uttering those verbal bombshells which are best unspoken He played this part of the free lance, but mind, an unpurchasable one, till 1865, in which year his wife presented him with a third child, a little girl, whose arrival mysteriously stirred his inmost heart. With his first two children he had experienced but a placid, tranquil joy : they lacked that gift which opens the heart of a father and completes the happiness of the household. Both won the affection but not the love of the old war-horse. They had far from realized the father's anticipations. Instead of the son of his dreams being a fine child, a bouncing rascal, a merry imp, one of those daring, restless younkers in whom old soldiers live their youth over again

and smell congreves in their squibs under the
laundry copper, the colonel found a wise, sen-
sible "little man," as he called him, and it was a
source of much melancholy, not unmixed with
shame, that his heir should be a precocious prig,
who never tore his trousers to scale a tenter-hooked
wall, or brought a farmer up to the house
against the young master who pelted him with
his own crabs, or came home dripping from saving
a kitten from the horsepond, or bleeding from a
combat with the village bully who would mock at
his humane reproof at the pound-dog being set
at some velocipede rider.

He experienced much the same feelings towards
his daughter, who was one of those little mothers
born to "teach a class." She seemed to play
with him only because it was her duty to amuse
him, and it apparently did amuse him. Indeed,
she might be said to have had no infancy at all,
and at the age of five, on the occasion of a gentleman visitor being expected, she would bustle to
be dressed scrupulously as for a parade. She had
a fear of her frock being crumpled by a father's
fondlings. Thus doubly repelled, even driven to
war adventures abroad, as mentioned, and for so
long a time storing up and concentrating his
affections, the colonel hastened to lavish them
over the cradle of the newly-born, whom he called
Marcia. He passed his time with "little Marsie," in the most charming tomfooleries. He was

continually streaming out her silky hair, like a
cornet playing with the horse-hair of his first
dragoon helmet. There was not a barrack-room
prank and antic, not a quaint word which he had
heard the men's wives utter over the washtub
not a scrap of semi-religious, wholly droll song of
the negroes in America, that he did not repeat
and act to keep her pretty rosebud mouth on the
laugh. He would weigh her despite the nurse's
superstitious remonstrance, and when she did not
wink at pulling the string that exploded a miniature cannon he had constructed of a pistol barrel
on a mount of wood, the servants thought the
master had gone mad. He would rise in the
depth of night to gaze on her sleeping, and spent
hours listening to that first breathing of child
life, so much resembling the exhalation of a
flower. When she awoke, he caught her first
smile, and if her tears, few and far between, had
but petrified, he would have worn the string of
them as a bracelet. Thus was he in a constant
bliss ; a sort of sentinel proud he was set to
guard a little angel.

What pleasures he enjoyed with her at Rugemound! He would drive her round the house in a
little goat carriage, looking down, as he marched
behind, every moment to see her shouting with
laughter, with the sun on her cheek, and her little
rosy foot bending double in her hand. Or he would
carry her on his walks, choosing frequented ways

now and the busiest hours, to let the child kiss her
hand to those who saluted them ; or, entering a
farmhouse, would exhibit his daughter's teeth.
On the way home the child would often slumber
in her father's arms as if he were a nurse. The
tears would dim his eyes when he recalled a hundred instances of a dying comrade's last cry, dis-
regarding the death agony : " Remember my little
one in England ; " and once, in a rare visit to
London, where he accidentally saw an Isabey or
Gerard painting of Napoleon making a similar fool
of his imperial self over the infant king of Rome,
he bought it only, apparently, to take the worth
of his money out of it in prolonged contemplation, terminating with a heartfelt, " Poor old
Boney ! "

When Marcia could run about fairly, out she
must trot with him into Elmwood; and there, under
trees full of song-birds, in the evening hours when
their voices are heard above the tortuous pathways, he would experience the ineffable joy of
listening to his child, who, moved by the melodious concert around her, would essay imitative
notes in murmuring and stammering, as if replying to the birds, and carrying on a parley in
a language not understood by men.

Somehow this last child was not so welcome to
Mrs. Pleasanton. Though a good enough wife
and mother, she was quite carried away by that
pride of the purse. She had been content with

two children, and the third was even unwelcome because it disturbed the others' expectations, and especially because it encroached on the heir's additional due. To her mother, this little girl foretold a division of land and of property, and hence a diminution in the importance of the family and a loss of social position.

Soon she began to leave her husband no rest ; the mother of the family was constantly attacking him as a politician, reminding the supine father that it was his duty to improve the fortunes of his increasing family ; what sufficed for two was inadequate for three. She even tried to separate him from old friends, and to undermine his fidelity to his line of action, the detriment done the soldier afield by the spillers of red ink at home ; she begged him to burn all the papers about the Chinese War, since after such an interval everybody had forgotten the story that he had emulated Palikao in plundering the Emperor Ching-chang-chung, or whatever his name was.

What ! make friends with the Quill-driver, who allowed exhausted men to meet the foe on empty stomachs while stacks of food crowded the warehouses a few miles away, all because Quill-driver had a stall at the opera and must positively quit the office at his regular hour in order to dress. Before he would let the Circumlocution Office rejoice at his being gagged, the mould of the grave should silence him !

Had things been as before, he would have gone afar to get a few more notches in his Garibaldi-like blade ; but he loved the home where Marcia was enshrined.

No! he would not sell his principles; but wearied with the persistency of the cowardly, greedy woman, he resigned his seat, and, buying the Gratchley Works, came thither to dwell, hard by the means to triple his fortune.

That was fifteen years or so before the opening of our story. The children had grown up. The enterprise had prospered, and the Colonel was doing a world-famed business. His son was a barrister, his first daughter was married, and Marcia had a fortune in her purse as well as in her face.

CHAPTER III.

COLONEL PLEASANTON'S house, said the architect with profound conviction, was a family residence in the Italian style. A vague description, which left one who had not seen it to have a vibrating mirage of a structure anything between a reduced Genoese palace and a *Parc Monceau* Renaissance bijou abode.

On leaving the boat, Marcia Pleasanton and her brother Henry, who was the dulcet youth who had spoken with Mr. Carroll Rendall, the chemist, paired off with Mr. Varney, the manager of the Works, thanks to whose influence he had lately entered the establishment, though his youth would have been an obstacle to anybody but one like Pleasanton, who had had his British prejudice against that Pitt-like defect amply obliterated.

The party of four, on entering the mansion, found several gentlemen connected with the Works or neighbouring residents, talking in a subdued tone like our tourists at a Swiss *table d'hôte*, where their English is understood by the Americans, and their French (a more difficult matter) by the poly-lingual waiters.   The large drawing-room, which was hung in Japanese chintz, and gay with showy-leaved plants and bright flowers, held in little baskets fastened on the curtains, and birds'-nests with their original proprietors stuffed and set on spiral wires. Near the fire-place Mrs. Pleasanton was welcoming, with every demon-stration of affection, her son-in-law and daughter, the Pryse-Prices, who had also just arrived. She deemed it incumbent on her, with witnesses by, to make a display of family affection and exhibit her maternal love.

The bustle of the embraces of the lady of the house and her wedded daughter was scarcely over before an old gentleman, so restricted in bodily dimensions that one fancied his old-fashioned black suit had shrunk him up, as the suddenly chilled tire contracts the wheel, who had, quietly as a fox, entered the room, saluting the hostess with a Regency bow as he passed her, walked straight to the group of which Mr. Rendall formed one, with a quite-at-home-already air revealing a good deal of the young chemist's worldly experience.

This little gentleman had a ferret face amid white whiskers, and carried a portfolio under one arm.

"What is that? what, what is that, sir?" he queried feverishly, as the scientific gentleman ceased speaking. "You call picture sales the best art galleries? and you know something about out-of-the-way art! He, he! Now come, come, sir, come," he ran on, hurrying him to the window, where he opened the cases and showed him a print, with a half-guarding action of the disengaged hand as if to prevent the treasure being snatched. "Do you know the name to give that, eh, eh?"

"That? Don't I though. 'Tis Mr. Garrick personating his murdered friend; an uncatalogued Hogarth, for I think more than ever it is our Englishman's work, though engraved in part by some foreign hand."

The little gentleman smiled delightedly.

"Never more were you right. I'll prove it some day! a Hogarth truly. But look"—he partly opened the portfolio again, but in such a grudging way that Rendall could barely thrust in a glance. "Proof before letters. Before letters, this is, do you see?"

"And on the Prince de Ligne's paper! whew!"

"And what margins! I do reckon this a gem. But I have not had it for nothing, the robbers! I had to bid high, for which I have to thank a woman."

"Indeed! They are becoming collectors now, it is so."

"She asked to have it handed her every time I

bid.   The cunning auctioneer kept saying: 'Let
the lady see it, Tim!'   At last I had it knocked
down at six pounds ten.   And what do you think
Miss Impertinence wanted it for? and in the first
place what do you think she was? an opera
bouffe singer! she wanted it to cut it up"—in
horror—"to cut the *Demi-Louison's* figure out as
a model for a costume!"   He closed the portfolio
as if he heard Miss Spangleigh's coming with the
scissors of the Fate.   "In my time actresses took
the costume as by the manager provided!   Have
another look!"

"Only to see one thing—yes!   I am right!
Milletone has another copy—"

"No! never!"

"Oh, Lord, yes! if you are very much set on
having the pair in the same frame—the French
Rothschild frames them so, you know—I daresay
I could get it you.   Milletone is not a painter that
cares for the Bosses.   D'ye see, he had my
advice—chemical analysis and all that—on per-
manent colours, and I would only have to ask
him."

"Ever so many thanks.   But is his before
letters, like mine?   Are you quite sure of that?"

"Speaking from memory, yes.   Before letters,
ay, but farther advanced than yours.   I swear that
arm is uncorrected—awfully out, is it not?"

"Splendidly incorrect."

"And the 'ici on attend'—ha, ha, ha."

The sentence which Rendall finished in the old collector's ear caused his lips to moisten and his cheek to glow with pleasure.

At this moment the colonel came in with his daughter in her dinner dress. He gave her his arm, on which she leant with a caressing and indolent air, her head thrown somewhat backwards, and gently rubbing her hair against his sleeve, like a kitten carried in arms.

" Good-day, everybody and company," said she as she kissed her sister and shook hands with her brother-in-law, and then running over to the gentleman with the portfolio cried : " May I peep at the treasures, godfather ? "

" No, my girl, they are not pictures you would care one fico for. But I have a volume of Rembrandt reproductions for you, honey," giving her a friendly fillip on the cheek.

" Upon my word, it is a most puzzling thing what a plenitude of pictures there are that one can never see ! " sighed Marcia, pouting and turning her back on the old man, who tied the port-folio strings with those Gordian knots familiar to the fingers of print collectors, and imitated from the intervoluted cords which the dextcrous De Brys delighted in complicating, to the despair of any copyist but the photographer.

" What is that I hear ? " suddenly exclaimed Mrs. Pleasanton, turning towards her daughter.

She had astutely decoyed Mr. Percy Goddard

upon a chair so near her that her dress touched him almost caressingly, for Mr. Percy Goddard, a young gentleman with a swarthy complexion which indicated Gipsy or Jewish ancestors, and muddy grey eyes, was the husband Mrs. Pleasanton hoped to secure for her younger daughter.

" What do I hear ? that you were carried further than ever you dreamt possible by the current. Why not say the tide ? I never heard of any current on the waste-water ! I fear you have been in some danger. I am at a loss to understand why your father allows—"

" My dear," replied the colonel, as, beside his daughter, he turned over the leaves of an album of contemporaneous celebrities on the table, with that indifference excusable towards marvels who are eclipsed daily by the newest hero discovered by the special correspondent, ' I should be sorry to know that a child of mine was afraid upon a watercourse which a kangaroo would take in its stride—its cruellest creature is a water-rat with no more whiskers than the modern cigarette-smoking young man ! "

" But I can assure you, mamma,"— it was Henry Pleasanton who glided in his soothing syrup,—" I assure you, there was no danger. They were carried a short distance by the current, and Mr. Rendall preferred drifting home in the side-wash to pulling briskly. They ought to have had Job with them. That's all."

D

Marcia, at this amiable remark, could but glance towards the object; but the chemist, though he happened to be looking that way, never winced, but went on contributing his part to a babble where Mr. Perch's shrill voice rang the changes upon an octave of Lancret, St. Aubin, Hervieu, and similar small bells.

"You drive away my uneasiness," graciously responded Marcia's mamma, whose countenance became as composed as the chemist's had never ceased to be. "But Marsie is so ungovernable, that I am always upon thorns. Why, look! her hair is quite wet."

"Done on purpose, mamma, to cool my head. I lost my hat, and was afraid of a sunstroke!"

"Mr. Bushrod!" announced a servant.

"One of our neighbours, whom you have not seen," whispered the hostess to Mr. Goddard.

"Well, how's the plantation, Dick?" inquired the colonel, of the new guest, as they shook hands.

"Flourishing like a green bay-tree. Three hundred new stakes set in to-day."

"Three hundred?"

"Three hundred, sir. That's not doing badly, I think. From the conservatory, you remember, I am cutting right down to the ornamental water, on account of the view. Only a fifteen-inch fall. If we were on the ground, I should have no need to explain it to you here. On the other side, you know, I raise the walk three feet. When that has been done, colonel, there will not be one square inch of my ground unturned ! "

" But when are you going to plant, Mr. Bushrod? " asked Marcia, preternaturally solemn. " Here you have had workmen in your garden for—oh, quite three years! Am I to be a gray-haired grandam without seeing even a two-year high sapling in it ? "

" Oh, trees ! they're the second consideration ; they're nothing. They can be planted at any time. More important matters take the prefer-ence ; for instance, the plans, the preparation of the land, by which in time, in good time, we get to putting in the trees."

Some one had entered by an inner door, who bowed without being noticed, and stood among the company before any one perceived him. He wore an honest countenance beneath a head of hair bristling like one of those hedgehog pinholders when full, which adorn a writing-desk. He was cashier of the Works, Mr. Boulter.

" We are all here ; Boulter's come," observed the head of the house, as he perceived this last addition. " Will you order dinner, Lotte ? These wrestlers with the waste-water Maelstrom must be sharp-set."

The murmur of the prelude to dinner was now at an end, and the grating of the spoons in the soup-plates was followed by a slightly more animated conversation.

"Mr. Goddard," began the hostess, who had placed the matrimonial candidate on her right, and made much of him, with a politeness which seemed almost oppressive. Her face was all smiles, and her voice was not like her usual voice at all, being her state reception voice, which made even the veteran butler nervous. Her glance wandered perpetually from the gentleman under her wing to his plate, and from his plate to his particular servant, whose anxiety approached that of a martyr on a burning ploughshare. It was the mother angling for a son-in-law, not yet cast in bronze—nothing but brass will meet the subject to be done by the realistic sculptor. "Mr. Goddard, we met one of your acquaintances the other day, Lady Seneschawl, who (in a stage whisper) betrayed one of your good actions."

Mr. Henry Pleasanton, who was studying the chemist furtively, pricked up his pointed ears; for a "good action," in which Goddard was engaged, might be worth his attention. But, in a moment his hopes were annihilated, and he washed down a bitter re flection on the ambiguities of our language.

"Yes, ye-es," said Mr. Goddard recovering his eyeglass, and disengaging it of a sprig of tanagon after it, both in the soup. Astonishing how the *monocle* will scoop up a quantity of that same vegetable without difficulty, though you might

chase it around for twenty minutes with the spoon
without securing enough timber to make a Queen
Mab chariot. " I had the pleasure of meeting the
Seneschawls in Italy. I was even fortunate
enough to be of some service to my lady."

" Did you rescue her from brigands ? " inquired
Marcia, with the guileless gush of a feeder upon
bygone romances.

" No, no ! a far less lofty matter. The lady
had a difficulty about a hotel bill, at the Hotel of
the Three Emperors and Borodino's. She was
alone, and I prevented her being plundered.
They will add in the number of rooms in your
suite with the items if they can ! "

" Well, I call that a robber's legend," commented Marcia.

" The least little thing," remarked Rendall,
already in the current as to the standing of
the dark-complexioned pet of the hostess, " will
do for a literary man !—why not get one of
those fellows to make an operetta of it, with
music by—Clay for example: I see a pleasant
piece for private theatricals ! A lady in distress,
between the puffy landlord and a horde of
waiters, presenting their bill, with the gendarme
and syndic in the background, when, suddenly
as St. Nick among the robbers, the young
English hero intervenes, points out the seven
francs fifty overcharged, and makes a triumphant
exit with my lady on his arm."

The colonel so much as winked and wined with him, while Henry gently bit his lip. But Mrs. Pleasanton, ignoring the long interpolation, went on purringly :

"Lady Seneschawl is a very agreeable woman. I never, I don't think, saw a more charming person. She has an expressive countenance. You know her ladyship, Perch ? " said she turning towards Marcia's art-loving godfather.

"Yes, I know the woman to be most agreeable," he answered in a forked sort of response, which took the gilding off the ladyship somehow.

" Oh ! godfather, she's the image of a satyr !" cried Marcia ; but observing a general smile at this strong simile, she felt herself blushing, and added quickly : " Oh ! of course I mean only as to the antique cameo—"

"That's what I call knocking yourself down before you have been picked up," commented Rendall to Mr. Perch.

" Were you any length of time in Italy, Mr. Goddard ? " asked the colonel, always dwelling on the name of Garibaldi's country for comradeship's sake, in order to turn the conversation.

" Oh, nearly half a year."

" What's your general impression ? "

" Interesting country for the eyes, repulsive to the nose " (this was his strong point, the assembly visibly granted), " exhaustive for the purse and palate. I could never bring myself to drink coffee out of glasses. The *maza-grand* is very different from Dick Swiveller's ' mazy.' "

"Italy ? " observed Henry Pleasanton, "I deem it the dullest, the least practical tour on Mr Cook's list. What obsolete agriculture ; what paltry ideas on trade. One day when there was a masked ball in Florence, I asked the restaurant waiter if they meant to keep open all night. ' Oh, dear, no, sir, we should have so many customers we should be driven frantic.' This is no fable. I heard the reply myself. That's enough to tell what a country is for business."

" I agree with Henry," chimed in Mrs. Pryse-Price, " Melrose Abbey, with a Burlington House Old Masters' Exhibition, and you have the antique side of Italy ; whilst for the modern it is the Boulevard des Capucines over again. Give me France, Paris ! you find such forethought and politeness there."

" Jackanape politeness," broke in Mr. Varney, louder than he intended. " As for their delicate forethought, it was a Scotch clerk of my acquaintance who put the Magasins of the Madeleine up to paper-bagging the coppers in change. Pish, forethought. Pooh, politeness."

Mrs. Pryse-Price nodded as if he had powerfully confirmed her opinion, and placidly proceeded :

" And their stuffs are so stylish, so immeasurably beyond—" Here a laugh from the quarter where Mr. Rendall was seated, drew her attention thither.

" Only Mr. Rendall," explained the colonel, " telling of a lace manufacturer in the North, who sends all his fabrics to Paris, whence they are packed back to London, so as to be guaranteed direct from the Rue St. Denis.   Oh, you deluded victims of the shopman ! "

" Well, then," returned Mrs. Pryse-Price, standing firm as a wild cat on the extreme end of the last bough left to her, " they still maintain supremacy for taste in making up material, I don't care where it comes from."

" Mr. Worth is an Eng—"

" Oh, we all know about Mr. Worth, sir," she replied to the colonel.   " I am speaking of Monsieur Vertugandin.   He made me an elegant mantilla à l'Infanta Don Felipe—resplendent with steel and *noir de Léonardo* bugles, that intense black, my dear ; and it required alterations. Would you believe me ?   He sat in an easy-chair with a long gilt folding-rod, not unlike the telescopic electric lamp-lighter, while I walked up and down before him with a woman at hand with a lump of scented chalk ; the French chalk was actually perfumed with the very rare Arabian flower, the *couscouscou !* "—here Colonel Pleasanton nearly choked himself at the colliding of a mouthful and a laugh—" and, spying the defects with the eye of an eagle, he deftly touched the points where the woman made the requisite marks for the seamstress. And then the mantilla fitted like a—a—"

Her husband failed to apply a fitting simile, and the company took something perfectly applicable as spoken.

" A man of genius, but very expensive," said Mr. Pleasanton.

" I saw two of his *redingotes anglaises*,—ha, ha! on a pair of sisters at Sandown, lately," said Mr. Goddard. "They were beauties."

" I daresay they were," uttered the colonel, not sorry Marcia and the chemist were arguing with Mr. Perch about aqua fortis. " It strikes me that between men and women dandies, there is little to choose. I heard of a West-end tailor retiring last week with a pretty plum ! "

" And I," added Rendall, " of an East-end slop-seller retiring with over eight hundred thousand. A *screw* makes its way—though there's a variation in time—in any material. I think you will find, however, that these fortunes are not strictly acquired in trade, but by money-lending." Strange to say the words seemed a poisoned shaft as well to Goddard as to Mrs. Pleasanton, innocent as the phrase sounded. As the swindler said to the magistrate, who really pitied so engaging a young gallant brought up for the fourth or fifth time, ' Well, your worship, if it were not for these annoyances '—he waved his handcuffs towards

the detectives—'thieving would be the finest trade
going.'"

"Ah! this is a capital *croûte aux champignons*,"
chuckled Mr. Bushrod—"a perfect picture; your
cook has surpassed him or herself; she's a first-rate
artiste. I shall remember her at Christmas, depend
upon it, with your leave, Mrs. Pleasanton."

"Why, I thought you never ate mushrooms,"
answered the hostess, pleased.

"Not in my own house, for I have my cook
under warning. I would offer no temptation—
would not have toad-stools—tears of repentance."

"Harriet," proceeded Mrs. Pleasanton, to her
married daughter, "I must take your husband to
task for neglecting us. We have not seen you for
over three weeks, Mr. Pryse-Price!"

"Bless me! my dear mother, if you only could
guess how busy I have been! you know how
George and I often work together! His father is
on committee in the House of Commons, and all
the business devolves on George. There are
hundreds of things only to be entrusted to confidential persons, friends rather than *employés*—
for instance, the launching that company to transport a floating palatial hotel all around the coast,
so that you spend a few days in each watering-
place during the season. Ah! all women are not
content with sitting at home over fruitless occupa-
tions. We shall realise a fortune out of that enterprise next summer; and then we shall buy a whole

territory in West America and colonize with—it's almost a State secret!—with the organ-grinders; thus," she concluded, repeating the prospectus, no doubt, "relieving the sensitive ear in London of what, nevertheless, would people the wilderness with harmonious sounds."

"I wish,' remarked Mr. Pryse-Price, "that we could include the old opera singers. That poor old ghost, Madame Scalinetta, worries me so, that I have not had a tenth of the value of my ticket the whole season."

"Oh, singing is out of date. We are going to have a revival of the ballet," said Goddard ; "and high time too! It is a fact. La Buoyante will come to Covent Garden next opening. They are going to revive *Les Quatre Saisons*, and Mr. Pitman, who is about the only musician who remembers the score, says it will be magnificent."

"What *début* were you speaking of?" asked Perch, a little aroused to hear of old times, of a-"Bunn"-dance, as the musty joke goes.

"La Bradizzi," answered Goddard.

"Ah! La Bradizzi, she is wonderful!" exclaimed Mr. Pryse-Price ; "we saw her in Milan. Such grace, such airiness! You don't even hear her steps when she is dancing."

"She's been the pet of La Scala, all her life," continued Goddard, trying to monopolize the topic, which gradually froze Mrs. Pleasanton.

" She speaks English with an Irish flavour,"
said Colonel Pleasanton. " I knew her in Naples,
or at least her manager dined with me, in the
bower of La Antonia, where the American consul
planted the cypress-vine which grew like the fairy
beanstalk."

" She ought to speak Irish," interposed Rendall, smiling ; " for Miss Brady is a genuine bog-
trotter, and learnt her art from a New York jig
dancer, my teacher on the banjo. I have seen her
as a girl, in a music-hall there."

Somehow or other, a Miss Brady did not seem
so well calculated to startle London as Signorina
La Bradizzi, and Goddard dropped the subject,
and sat mute, staring indignantly at the destroyer
of his celebrity.

" We expected you last evening, Henry," said
Mrs. Pryse-Price, to her brother, conceiving an
aversion to the chemist for having graduated in
banjo play.

" I was at my debating club," was the reply.

" Henry has been appointed speaker," said Mrs.
Pleasanton, proudly enough.

" Dear me !"

" Ah," said Perch, " the Chatham Club. Is it
still going on ? I liked that little speechifying
society when I was young. How many do you
number ?"

" Two hundred."

" And all statesmen in embryo ! What an

alarming prospect for the nation.   What did you debate upon ? "

" A proposal to make yachts available in case of war as *avisos*, despatch boats, and even as privateers—one big gun, fire at long bowls, and flit away ! "

It was indubitably an expression of contempt which passed over the speaker's father's face, and, as if to obtain the reply which the colonel sought, and yet dreaded, Mr. Rendall inquired :

" Have you a vessel suitable ?"

" No.   If we form the association, I am to be chairman of the committee to contract for the guns ; the—ahem, commissions will be weighty enough ! " he openly avowed, with a smile of self-approval, reflected on Goddard as faithfully as from a satellite.

" You do well," exclaimed the latter, just stopping short of drumming applause on the edge of plate with his cream spoon.

" You mean he will do well," gruffly appended the colonel, tickling himself with the long ends of his moustache, as he contracted his facial muscles, like an old soldier biting a particularly tough cartridge.

" I like to encourage all such things," pursued the younger Pleasanton, " and not to counteract the laws."

Rendall laughed outright.

" Who told you that ? " cried he to Henry.   " I

see you are making me your target. Since my cousins, if they are my cousins, will go trumpeting the very natural action, you may as well lay the storm of curiosity you have excited."

"Very natural action," said Mr. Henry Pleasanton, gravely, as became a future Attorney-General, or whatever his mark might be. "It is a simple affair. A gentleman died in Australia, where he had wedded his wife's sister, and left you, on an assertion of relationship, all his home property, but you handed it over to his children."

"Very well."

"Now, that's what I call an illegal wrong, a deplorable action. What is the intent of the law? One quite clear. It is that parents should be punished by their children born out of wedlock being incapable of inheriting property. You knew this very well; your legal adviser must have told you. And yet, what have you done? You enrich the children! you set at defiance the law, the spirit of the law, everything established by sages! Giving up the fortune in this way, Mr. Rendall, though you had the philosopher's stone in your crucible, is to shock propriety, to encourage immorality!"

"My dear sir, all know your rigid principles where Father Antic, the law, is concerned; but what else, as a man, would you have had me do? When I saw those poor boys, three of them, I said to myself that I could never enjoy life again if my path was paved with their coin. I do not believe there was even one of the Stoics perfect ! "

" But that pretty talk is not the law. When the wisdom of our predecessors says a thing, it has some object in view, you must grant. The law is against such ill-timed generosity. Supposing others imitated you ? "

" No fear of too many doing such things, Henry," said the colonel, who had never called his son " Harry," and could not have done so now for a king's ransom.

" We ought never to set a bad example," continued Pleasanton, sententiously. And turning towards the chemical expert, he added, " Bear in mind, Mr. Rendall, I don't esteem you the less for what you have done ; on the contrary, I render homage to your disinterestedness. But as for shouting ' Well done, thou good and faithful steward,' no, no, not I. You act on fits and starts too much, dear fellow ; and yet, with that large sum you diverted, and steadiness, you might have laid the foundation of a fortune ; with your talent, you might be—well, I do not know but you could be Secretary of the Home Department."

Mrs. Pleasanton gave the chemist a long look, much more favourable than heretofore. She was surprised at her son patronising the man.

" I have been something greater than Home

Secretary," returned Rendall, quietly, with a twinkle in the eye, which glanced towards Marcia.

"Greater !" echoed Henry, eyeing him with astonishment.

"Seriously," resumed the chemist, "I have had far more splendid prospects. What do you say to Dictator to the Government of France?"

CHAPTER IV.

WHILE THE SERVANTS ARE IN THE ROOM.

"YOU laugh," continued the young professor, "and you may open your eyes, but if you will kindly repeat that operation with your auricular appendages, you may have the substance on which to pronounce your judgment. I was lodging in the Rue Chapelle-Ardente in Paris, when the siege detained me, and I was in the same place when the Commune ruled the roast. One day I was quite at a loss what to do with myself—when you have participated, more or less voluntarily, in the taking of the Tuileries in the morning, you do not feel much like humdrum occupation for the rest of the day. However, my stroll took me to the old Myers' Circus buildings on the Place de la République, and there being an unpleasant crowd on the plaza, I stepped into the broad coach gateway, and seeing a stairway invitingly on the yawn, like myself, I began to mount it, and finding a room door open also, it occurred to me that I could look out of the window of this front room on the multitude, a very agreeable position for a scientific student, who has no yacht to carry a long

E

Tom and blaze destruction at a merchantman nine miles away. In case of a charge of cavalry, it is noteworthy with what philosophical calmness you scrutinize the line they keep if you are on the first story of a tall house. The room was a sort of office, fitted with book-case and writing desks, but untenanted; a couple of Gras bullets on the blotting-pad, fallen after flattening on the gaselier, seemed to suggest the reason of the latest occupant having left me the end of his lease, and also that looking out of window in a country where the infantry always fire at a face behind the blinds, was misspent curiosity. So I sat down at the desk and set to picking one of the bullets out of the pad with the penknife, to rest myself and wait till the mob left me free to go to the little café in the Rue de Bondy, where the proprietor always found something to put before his theatrical patrons—if only a 'property' fowl. I am not boring you? Thanks, so much. I found a cigar case, and as one who smokes, lunches, if not dines, I was smoking like a green wood fire, when a gray gentleman entered. He saw me sitting, and thought I belonged to the place. He had no hat, and I thought the house belonged to him. He asked me very politely if I could understand English, and as I ventured to answer that I could, he desired me to put into that noble tongue a proclamation for the benefit of the British in the Opera end of the town who had any money, and provisions, and arms, guaranteeing recompense after the Versailles troops and the Prussians should be repelled from the profaned soil of Liberty. He thought my handwriting and the eye-catching way I arranged the stirring lines very pretty, and when I interpreted the sentences, *proclaimed* me, not publicly, of course, the pearl of secretaries, and there and then engaged me! I had dictated to the chief of the Commune *pro tem.* I am careful to impress the *pro tempore* upon you, for I learnt he was shot in Père-la-Chaise, upon Molière's grave, the next day. At the same time, to be able to say that you dictated to the government of a country—or even city—is a feather in a humble gentleman's cap."

At this conclusion the colonel, pouncing upon a plate of cakes, saw fit to demolish the pyramid by taking one from the base.

"Francis!" called out his vigilant wife, "symmetry!"

"I beg your pardon, my dear! symmetry? you're right, I forgot," and he took the top cake.

"The colonel has a perfect mania for disorder. I never could understand why his men styled him a disciplinarian."

"I was wrong, my dear, wholly wrong. You see, friends, my wife is an indulgent woman save when symmetry is in question. Symmetry is one of my wife's 'articles of social war.'"

" How absurd you are, Mr. Pleasanton," said his wife, who had expected her mate to act upon her ocular signalling, and not draw her into speech, while blushing at being caught in such a flagrant exhibition of domestic economy.

There was no revenge possible but to take it out of her daughter. So, biding her chance, she suddenly shot a rocket over all the heads upon Marcia, who was listening to more ruddy pages of the Commune.

"Marsie, my dearest, your bracelet is unclasped, and you will drag over your glasses!" which set all attention on the girl's arms—rather too robust, she thought, in her aspiration to be an emaciated Umbrian nymph—and so calling up her colour.

CHAPTER V.

"GENTLEMEN," said the host, when they had returned to the drawing-room, "you know we may smoke. We have to thank my son for that; he has been so fortunate as to obtain the concession from his mother."

"Coffee, godfather?" asked Marcia of Mr. Perch.

"No," replied the collector. "I like my sleep."

"Here?" queried the Hebe, finishing the sentence for him before she accosted the cashier.

"I never take it, Miss Pleasanton, so many thanks."

She moved about here and there, amid the loungers, until there was no reply to her challenge: "Has every one been looked to?" and crossed in a sort of tragic-actress style, without any intention—but Rendall's tales of the heroic *petite Parisienne* had made her prouder of her sex—and struck up on the piano the prelude of a Hungarian gipsy waltz.

" Is anybody going to have a spin? I do like to play to the dancing."

" Will you let us smoke the pipe of peace in peace ?" cried her father.

" Yes, dearest Bear ! " But resuming her melody, she began dancing her toes on the pedals, without any music before her, her head turned towards the room, animatedly smiling with the excitement of the weird and brisk tune in her eyes, and soon following the cadence with her figure. Her shoulders swayed to and fro ; her body undulated as if her waist were clasped by the arm of a partner ; her whole form indicated the varying measures of the dance ; but Rendall's eyes dwelt too markedly upon her, and she turned again to the piano ; her head softly nodded time, while her eyes followed her hands as they flew along the ivories. Now she struck the notes, now she caressed them, or would speak to them, scold them, smile on them, fondle them, lull them to sleep. She rolled forth bold passages that made the colonel think of drum and bugle ; she toyed with the melody— now with tenderness, then with passionate nerve ; the strain sank and soared again, as the top of her pearl-headed tortoise-shell comb, in the Spanish style, now shone in the light, and now was concealed in her dark tresses. The wax tapers in the piano sockets vibrating with the fingering, flashed on her profile, or mingled their lights upon her more prominent features. The shadow of her ear-rings, two coral balls, fluttered on her neck, like a bewildered hawk-chased bird; while the long pliant fingers ran so quickly over the black and white, that Rendall could hardly follow them.

"It is something out of her own head," said the colonel to Goddard.

"She had lessons from the Russian demon-pianist," added his wife, whispering the amount of the cheque paid to the same gentleman.

"There! so finishes the music!" cried Marcia, waking up to the consciousness that she had gradually encompassed the whole audience, and leaving the instrument, to place herself opposite Mr. Rendall. "Tell me a story, something more about lively Paris, to amuse me, Mr. Rendall; anything you know—your telling it will make it desirable to hear."

She stood erect before him, like a suppliant slave after Gérôme; her arms folded, her head a little thrown back, the whole of her body leaning on one foot, with more sauciness than a suppliant air, and a kind of roguish impudence which en-hanced the somewhat free and easy grace of her costume. It was a broad Vandyke amber lace collar over a white velvet corsage, with a coffee-and-cream dress, trimmed heavily with beads, ruby, black and amber.

"When will you cut your wisdom tooth, my

friend ?" asked the chemist, with a gravity rather
beseeming his occupation than his mood.

" Never," she replied, beginning to laugh.
" Well, where's my story ? "

Rendall looked round to see if any one was
listening, and lowering his voice, replied : " Once
upon a time there was a father and a mother who
rejoiced in a charming, yet marriageable daughter.
The papa and the mamma invited a rich gentleman
to their house, on matrimonial views intent ; but
the little child only snubbed him and kicked up
such a row on the piano that he thought Wagner
was her trainer, and ran away, and is running till
this day."

"How wicked you are ! That will do ; I am
going to take up my work."

And finding a fancy bag somewhere, where it
had no real excuse to be, she sat down by her
mother's side, as you see a lamb nestle by the
dam when a railway engine screams by the pasture
side.

" Are we to have no *euchre* this evening ' asked
the colonel, who had introduced more than this
American pastime among his intimates.

" Yes, if you like, my dear," said Mrs. Pleasanton, resignedly ; " the table is empty, as you may
see, and you have only to have the lights."

" Going, going, gone ! to Mr. Perch again. Mr.
Perch, too late," cried Rendall, into the ear of
the collector, dozing by the side of the fire-place,

and rolling his head about like a traveller in an express train which is trying to recover a lost twenty minutes.

The old gentleman started, the young one held out a playing card to him, with the words, "The King of Spades, early wood engraving, before letters. You are wanted at the card-table."

" Are you not too tired this evening, Miss Pleasanton, with your boating and all?" said Goddard, as he approached Marcia.

"Not I ; I feel as if I could dance all night."

" Ah, what do you call that lovely embroidery —a—a bag of mystery, eh ?   How pretty!"

" This ?   Oh, very, very, very pretty!"

She held up a shapeless nucleus of something in wool, but the more he looked at it, the less he could divine the object.

" Well, it's a sock, a baby's sock. I am knitting it for a poor little pet, in the Queen Anne style, with a rococo toe, as you see, a Chippendale foot, and a Cimabue border ; not to be bought in any shop, I assure you.   Embroidery, tapestry, tambour work —they demand attention.   But this—you see the fingers only are working—when once it is begun it goes on of its own accord, and leaves one at liberty to think of any nonsense that comes up."

" Marcia, dear," interjected her father, " can you not come here as my *mascotte*, my lucky-eye ? The more I lose the less I can get my money back."

"Bravo, el toro, encore the bull! I shall keep that for my collection of witticisms," replied Marcia. Then, glancing up at Mr. Goddard, who wished he had not approached her, and was wondering how he could get away nicely, she said, "Are you thinking of some speech to add to it? Oh, Mr. Rendall, I wish you would cease to put out papa with your evil eye, and bring yourself here! I'm wearing coral, and I am not a jot afraid of you. No, no, I mean nearer."

Mr. Goddard and Mr. Rendall were thus brought side by side. Goodness knows what demon prompts the caprices of a young lady given to mischief, but Marcia was startled at the contrast she had inadvertently brought about.

"Mr. Rendall, as a chemist I take a pride in you, and I am not going to have our Works presided over by gentlemen out of the fashion. Look at Mr. Goddard with his hair so exactly divided in the centre like a Guido-esque angel! and you—I never saw a more horrid red Indian scalplock right in the middle of the forehead! Down on your knees, Sir; you do not surely expect me to stand on a chair to get at it? Down on your prayerless knees and—"

"Is that child mad?" cried Mrs. Pleasanton, just aware of what was going on, as Goddard backed out of the group.

"Miss Pleasanton," said Rendall, "I believe

you have taken vows to be the despair of your family! If I met a mine as full as you of quicksilver, I should be made for life?"

"Gently, Marsie, gently, my dear," said the colonel, very kindly indeed, for his vein had turned.

"So I shall deal with him gently," returned Miss Romp, playfully threatening the chemist with the scissors. "Now, beware! if you stir, your warlock is doomed, Sir Wild Chief of the Prairies. Do you cower? do you shrink, sir? Oh, coward, fie! But I cut hair very well, don't I, papa?" And, leaping up, she made one or two plunges with the scissors into Rendall's thick curls, and went to the fire-place to throw what she had really cut off into the grate.

"There!" she taunted him, "nicely you've been cheated, you thought I wanted to steal a love-lock from you."

She had paid no attention to her brother, who now coughed loudly; to her mother, who turned first crimson and then pale. Her father, laying his cigar on his cards, and rising from the card-table approached her with an air rather of embarrassment than vexation. She eluded him, pounced on his cigar, put it to her lips, gave one puff, threw it away very quickly, turned aside her head, coughed, blinked like a bull-terrier in for a scolding, and exclaimed:

"And smells so, *pa!* now don't you make it as

hot for me as that on my tongue, dear old papa !"
crossing her arms after the old picture in her room ·
of Jenny Lind in *Robert the Devil*, and bowing
her head like *Milady* when the executioner
engaged by Monsieur Athos was about to deal his
stroke.

Colonel Pleasanton stood irresolute. Rendall
burst out into an irrepressible laugh.

In the tumult, Mr. Perch woke up, and Mrs.
Pleasanton steering to cut off Marcia before she
eluded her at the door, said in a stern and sorrowful voice :

" Was ever such behaviour ! Really something must be done with you ! What ails you
this day ? I never saw your match ? "

" I have," muttered Rendall. " *Ego !* please
Heaven, it will be I."

CHAPTER VI.

"A QUARTER past ten already!" said Mrs. Pryse-Price; "we shall have barely time to catch the train. Marcia, let the maid bring me my wraps."

Every one rose from tea. Mr. Perch woke up from dreams of an immaculate Sandrart in the first state, and the little cohort of guests from town prepared to depart for the station.

"I shall run out with you," said Mr. Rendall. "I stand in need of a blow."

Mr. Goddard looked as if he could oblige him, in one sense of the word, with exceeding relish.

Perch went first, giving his arm to the mutterer. Mr. Pryse-Price followed, and Henry and the chemist brought up the rear, a sort of couple which a young cuirassier and a sutler's clerk would have formed.

"Why don't you stay the night here? You could go up in the morning," suggested the man of the laboratory.

"No," replied the other, "can't be 'did.' I have to fall to work first thing to-morrow. I can

nap in the train, and get a good sleep, and tackle my
work fresh as a judge home from a long vacation."

They walked on silently. Every now and then
a word from old Perch reached them. He was
sounding the praises of his god-daughter to her
suitor.

" The old gentleman is very sanguine," was the
gloss of Henry. "Don't you agree with me,
Carroll, that it's no match ? "

" I have not been long enough here to pronounce on family matters."

" My dear fellow, what rubbish ! you have eyes
and ears ! Will you tell me, by the way, why
you encouraged my sister in all her fantastics this
evening ? You have already obtained considerable
influence over her, and—"

" I ? My good boy," said Rendall, puffing his
cigar as regularly as a machine, "allow me,
between brackets, so to say, to begin with a social,
scientific and philosophical disquisition : we—by
which ' we ' I mean the majority of the men I
know and care to touch elbows with, who are
neither for tabernacle nor theatre, but are working
off superfluous steam before we settle down into
the regulation stroke—we have come to the conclusion to have done for ever with the young lady
brought up in the primitive school, which should
have been strangled in its own shoe-ties that
crossed in the front and went twice round ere
they meet for tying. In Sailor William's reign

the men spent their leisure over port and other heady liquors, and to meet Miss Primlily, who squeaked 'Mamma, may I?' and 'Please, papa!' as the *ingénue* still does in a Palais-Royal first piece, was a diversion. We want something more like the American heiress, of whose specimens we are inundated in this decade, bar the voice of piccolo piercingness and the too brilliant piano playing. Thank the saints, there's nothing in womanhood to equal the English girl, when you let her develop her ever-just and honourable impulses. It is delightful to find parents owning their predecessors' blunders, for now they engage thorough proficients to teach her the royal roads to be a husband's pride as well as delight. She acquires the artistic manner; can pull up that deucedly impudent French maid, who used to guide her young mistress's tastes; and we are amazed when she comes out in some garden with her sisters and makes Chantilly turn pale!"

"Marcia goes nowhere, and has no need to invent telling toilettes. Have you done, without a tail to your speech?"

"Now," went on Rendall, without replying to him, "add to this, modern education, an indulgent father, good-nature and tenderness embodied, encouraging girlish spontaneity by his weakness and adoration; suppose that this father has winked at the idle pranks of a sort of amateur Cherubino; has allowed his daughter to wear a mad-cap over a sufficiently wise head, in which is a brain quite after his own pattern—"

"But how comes it that you, my friend, who are wise beyond your years, famous among your colleagues, appreciated in Germany even, who have seen my sister at home of late, and the way she has been brought up, the manners acquired from presuming on fatherly indulgence—in short, all that makes it so difficult to offer her as acceptable—how can you encourage her as you did this evening, to commit a series of scenes in the domestic circle—ladylike 'clowneries,'—when you might at once put a stop to them with one of those sentences which you, and you alone, as far as I know, can say to her—dare to say to her!"

"I dare a good deal, I hope, when the reason suffices. But I have no such influence as you imagine." His cigar being short, Rendall drew a rather large knife and held the transfixed stump upon it to obtain a couple more whiffs before casting it aside.

"There are times," resumed Henry, "when the tomfooleries of my sister are of no consequence, but this evening, before Mr. Goddard, who will break off the marriage, I am certain ; for he is not a fool, to be made a laughing-stock. A desirable alliance, if ever there was one ; for I have specially inquired. An excellent young fellow in every respect."

"Do *you* think so ? He positively disgusted

me, for your sister's sake ! And this is the reason
of my exercising none of the authority for reproof
which you attribute to me. That fellow," he added
letting his tongue wag, "if ever he loses his money,
and I have seen his vastly superior compeers lose
their all in a crash, he would sponge on all that
knew him for six months, and then it would be a
toss-up between becoming tout to a bill discounter
or decoy to a copper-hell. Were he a man, I should
not speak this way of him behind his back—but one
cannot face such a person with cool analysis ! Can
even a rustic mistake such veneer for solid wood
—he is the vulgarity of elegance ! a tailor's
dummy, mentally as well as physically ! I believe Dicky Chapone spoke the truth when he
said that he was in Krautunganse's the tailor's, and,
on being refused a renewal, and naturally a little
confused, nudged a lay figure in a suit, and said,
'Come along, Goddard, nothing to be done here.'
He a husband for your sister ! How the deuce
do you expect *him* to understand HER ? How can
he ever discover the noble, ardent, generous
nature which underlies her many eccentricities ?
Can you imagine a single idea in common between
them ? By George—and the Dragon !—had I the
ghost of a right to counsel, I should never object
were your sister to wed no matter whom, provided
he were intelligent, that he had some character, an
idiosyncrasy, anything capable of ruling or in-
fluencing such a woman's nature ! Very often the

F

worst faults of a man make a woman's heart beat:
they are an excess, an undue proportion of the Pro-
methean fire. I never set my eyes on a field of the
wildest oats without seeing some flower growing
there. Even to a rake a woman might possibly
become attached by Othello's failing; an ambitious
man, or a man of business, like yourself, would
give her occupation, and lure her into sympathetic
dreams of his future advancement. But union
with a contemptible money-lover like that! and
for ever! She would not snap one of her own hairs
in honour bound, but she would tug like
Prometheus against golden chains, until she rent
them! But you know that she is not of the
common herd of girls. Don't set such a pearl in
the window of a dealer in paste and Monte Carlo
jewellery. Find her a prince, my boy! there are
several crushed out of their kingdoms by Prussia ;
and hang me the day when her husband says she
looks or acts unworthy the diadem ! "

"But, Carroll, Goddard has something like
five hundred thou—"

" Henry, make haste, do," called out Pryse-
Price, from under the wooden verandah of the little
station.

" That's in the Puebla and St. Louis Railroad,
and three hundred thou— "

"I have your ticket ! Come on, the train is in."

And Carroll returned alone, cigarless, to the
colonel's.

He did go into the house, but he was one of those enviable men with whom servants are confidential without being disrespectfully familiar, and the butler warned him that Mr. and Mrs. Pleasanton were having a heated set-to in the drawing-room, so he marched away from the doorway, merely delaying to don his overcoat, and went to his own dwelling at an easy distance to cover.

CHAPTER VII.

MR. AND MRS. PLEASANTON were indeed in confab. The Saxony china time-piece had just struck twelve, deeply and slowly, as if to emphasize the solemnity of that hour for conjugal deliberation.

" Don't go to sleep, Francis ! "

It was the lady's non-company voice, and would have awaked him of Sleepy Hollow, or them of Ephesus.

" Never more attentive," was his reponse, but, all in the lazy tone of a man who, with his eyes still open, is beginning to feel the pleasure of the horizontal position, in which he was occupying three chairs like an American at a sea-side hotel, or a trooper after a day's ride.

" Oh, you are going to sleep ! "

" Never in a chair. Well, what is it ? "

" Oh, nothing unusual. I think Marcia's con-duct has been most unbecoming this evening, that's all. Did you notice it ? "

" No, I did not notice it. I was going to do

so, but Leester came in with the tea-tray, and she got away smiling."

"A dreadful action of hers. I wonder Mr. Rendall did not go away insulted. But, after all, that is not the point, for you could engage another chemical adviser. It is the cold shoulder she has turned upon Mr. Goddard. Henry says he is deeply hurt about it, and though the gentleman is not likely to refer to it, it is doubtful that we shall ever have him here again. And a man of thousands!"

"Rather a pig!" grunted the colonel, not unlike the animal itself. "But admitting he may retire his addresses out of fire, what is a man to do?" upon which the colonel, raising himself in the apex chair of the triad, stretched both his hands interlaced in front of him and then back over his head like an athlete. "Let him retire. He is not the only young and wealthy gentleman in the kingdom—plenty of them. Whilst girls like *my* daughter—"

"*Your* daughter, indeed! *your* daughter!"

"You never render her justice, Lotte."

"Do I not? I do all possible justice. But I see her in her true colours, not with your spectacles. She has faults, very great faults, which you have fostered, yes, you; she is giddy and capricious as a child of ten! Do you suppose I have not suffered from her fickleness and unreasonableness since we have been trying to get

her settled, and then she has such a way of dis-
posing of those who are introduced to her, so rude,
so mountebank-like. She is positively alarming,
distressing! Why, she has sent at least half a
score eligible men to the right about, as you
call it."

At these concluding words a flash of paternal
vanity lit up the veteran's eyes.

"Yes, yes," said he, smiling at the recollection; "the fact is, she has a deal — the de'il
of a spirit! Do you remember her painting
Widow Barnett's four children with yellow
ochre, and coming up the road with two in her
arms and one on each skirt, and crying out to
Mr. Willowweeds, who had been posing as a
Howard at the least, 'Don't come near me—it's
the jaundice!' He tumbled through the—ha, ha,
ha!—through the *ha, ha!* indeed "—and here
the colonel, who had never made so good a
joke in all his life, emitted another laugh so undeniably of the horse category that all the steeds
in a hussar barracks would have neighed in
unison if they had but heard him—" in his haste
to take the eleven forty-five for London!"

"Very amusing, truly," assented his wife ironi-
cally, "and highly commendable. Undomesti-
cated though husbands are nowadays, I still believe they would choose to see a cook-book in
their future wives' hand in preference to a practical joke-book! A little more of such spirit, as

you term it, and who will undertake to bottle our wasp?"

"For the sake of the honey?" began the colonel, who was decidedly in the humorous vein.

"A few more such proceedings, and how many proposals will your daughter receive? It seems the harder cross to bear after my having had no difficulty over Harriet."

Mr. Pleasanton made a face so wry that its return to its ordinary aspect seemed impossible.

"In short," was the continuation of the marrying mamma's diatribe, "the matter is important to the dear child. When she reaches thirty, after refusing every one worth having, when there will be no one to accept her in spite of all her wit and fine talent, then she will perhaps regret, and bemoan her folly, and so will you."

There was a pause, as the torturer gives his victim time to breathe. Mrs. Pleasanton allowed her husband a spell to beguile him into the belief that she had finished, then instantly changing her tone she proceeded: "I now have to speak to you of your son."

Hereupon the old soldier, hitherto indolent under the lash of his wife, raised his head, smiling faintly with good nature.

Everybody knows the different eyes with which a marrying mamma regards "the placing" of her offspring in the world according to their sexes; she wishes her daughters to have a position, and their happiness is a secondary consideration, but she aims at the sons being happy, whether on a lofty pedestal or not.

Mrs. Pleasanton's bearing to her boy had been remarked in two stages ; when he was an infant, she had disregarded him to a degree that earned her in the house the reproach of unnatural coldness; but all of a sudden, when some ten years had passed, she began to evince a devotion, anxiety and tenderness, fierce in their ceaseless outcome. She pardoned his faults before committed, backed him up against all else, sided with him, and spoilt him as the mamma's darling invariably is spoilt.

Henry would have been educated at home under private tutors ; but it chanced that the colonel was in England at the critical juncture, and he so passionately insisted on no more molly-coddling for his heir, that Mrs. Pleasanton had to dry her tears, and let the youth go away. All she could do was to see the tutor with whom he resided, and make his path smooth.

During the seven years he spent under that tutor's roof, a week did not pass without one day of it being devoted to a maternal visit.

Henry took kiss and tip, and forgot his mother before the first had evaporated.

When he came home, a finished gentleman, she acted like a Frankenstein who had created, not a monster, but an Adonis. She paid the college tradesmen's bills without letting even the solicitor audit them, and provided her son with ample funds to dress against viscounts coming of age. There was so strong an apish temperament in him that she was duped by his close assumption of style, and thought him the model man about town.

If ever she read one of those paragraphs in the Society journals which, if witty, are probably adaptations from some squibs upon the heroes of the *Gazette d'Amsterdam*, in 1750 ; and if stupid, are original fabrications, she would pretend to read between the lines and parade the blank she, logically, found there as her son. If he had been a Parisian and had fought a duel, she would have framed the pistol or rapier and set it where a shrine should be. His valet was not as other servants in her infatuated eyes.

She was no reader, her husband was too much absent to have taught her diversions to be shared with him; she had no turn as a devotee; no graces to win agreeable friends ; apparently afraid to make Marcia her companion, lest Henry should be jealous. She clung to her son so closely that Mr. W——, of Scotland Yard, who had occasion to stop three days in the house concerning a burglary, remarked : " I never saw such doating in persons of their age, natural affection not being forgotten, unless there was a bond of crime." Sinister sentence ! but crime was a ridiculous word in relation to a perfectly irreproachable married woman, and a young fellow beginning life without any dread of inability to gratify temptation.

At all events, Charlotte Pleasanton centred all her hopes in Henry's fortunes, all her pride in his future welfare.

Her sole thought by day and by night, her fixed star was to contrive such a rich and brilliant match for him as would recompense her for all the dreariness and gloom of her lonely existence.

"Do you even remember your son's age, Mr. Pleasanton?" resumed the maternal schemer.

"Henry! I'll tell you off hand! let me see, Henry ought to be—he was born in '53; that is, his age, I think—"

"You think! A pretty father you are, to ask! Yes, 1853, the 12th of July."

"When I ought to have been in the Crimea. Ah, ah! Well, we make him out twenty-nine. Yes, that's it."

"And with a son nearly thirty, you lean on your sword, while you ought to point out how he is to go into action. You don't trouble yourself about what is to become of him. You simply say : 'Yes, that's right, twenty-nine.' Any one else would bestir himself and would look about. Henry is not like his sister, but is bent on marriage. Have you ever thought of finding a wife for him ? No more than for the Emperor of China, whose tea service you brought home! It was just so with your elder daughter.

I should like to know what trouble you ever took about *her* marriage ! One would have supposed it was all the same to•you whether she found a husband or not. Wasn't I obliged to goad you before you would move in the matter ? Oh ! you rub your hands unfoundedly for that marriage, Your daughter's happiness should not be *your* consideration. I should like to know where you would have found a son-in-law like Pryse-Price without me ? a man who worships Harriet, and, though he is a man of the world, a model husband."

The listener, wondering if this lecture was going to usher the morning in, dozed again, with an involuntary vision arising of a Turk's head, which he had cleft in early practice, faithfully resembling the belauded absentee.

" Where," she tirelessly ran on, "where is the son-in-law who would be so attentive as he is to us ? With time so valuable to him, he actually spent no less than a couple of hours in the Burlington Arcade, matching the statuette of which your cane broke the pendant."

"Excuse me, my dear," ventured the roused worm at last, "what are we talking about ? I have some desire to snatch a little sleep to-night. You began with your son and your daughter. Now you are expatiating on the chapter of her husband's perfections ; they are as numerous as a Venezuelan Generalissimo's bulletins of the day—a chapter long enough to last till to-morrow

morning. Is there an end ? You wish your son
to marry ? Well, I am of the same mind ; let
him put the names of the·suitable ladies in a hat,
and pop—propose to them according to lot. I
have seen a life disposed of in a somewhat similar
mode."

"For shame, Mr. Pleasanton. You will joke
brutally, instead of lending me your aid."

"Not lend you my aid! You are the most
unjust woman ever created. I have put myself
out to cajole half a dozen guardians, and twice as
many papas ! The wretched wine, the hard-
mouthed cigars, the dull evenings I have submitted
to ! But I tell you that these wharfingers and
horse-dealers, and pirates, and rent-collectors who
have amassed money, only admire the dashing
six-footers who look down on them, slap them on
the back with a whack like a forty-pounder, con-
demn their smokes as poisonous, say plainly
they won't come again unless the wine is better,
and threaten to heave Aminidab Crozier out of the
window if he interrupts their spicy anecdotes of
driving the celebrities of the Casta Diva Theatre.
I am devilish sorry, but Henry is no more a
Hercules than a drummer boy !" and this last sentence he uttered with a feeling of regret which made
his hearer start, and murmur his name pleadingly.

"In short, sir, the truth is I am to blame for
everything. You make me out selfishness itself.
There, just like all you men."

" Thank you for the moustachio'd sex."

" Well, it is your nature, and what is the use in being angry with you for it. It is only mothers who torment themselves ! Oh, if you were a little like me, if you were always thinking of what may happen to a handsome young man ! I am well aware that Henry is cool-headed ; but there are so many designing, intriguing creatures ! we hear such cases every day. I should go mad, though ! Francis, suppose we—"

There was no reply, for the colonel had gone off into one of those soldierly slumbers which nothing but the *reveille* would interrupt. Out of feminine spite she left him there, in the chair, with his heels on the other two, like a dragoon poised on his spurs, turned off the gas with her own hands, so that no servant would come in to rouse him, and retired. It was the first stretch of repose he had had out of the trenches for years.

CHAPTER VIII.

THE colonel brought an appetite which would
have forced Gargantua to fear a rival was presented, to the breakfast table, where he made the
more hearty meal from the absence of his wife.
He and Marcia had it all to themselves, and were
gay as a pair of linnets.

Mrs. Pleasanton had gone to town.

" Where, did she say ? "

" To Mr. Wrench's."

" Oh! her dentist."

That explained all.

In America, when the lady of the house dis-
appears temporarily, it is given out that she has
gone to a matinée; in Catholic countries that
Madame is at confession; and in England that the
dentist is honoured; and no more can be said. It
is the clincher which drives the marital sphinx
to cast himself over the abyss of silent submission.

However, Mrs. Pleasanton's dentist dwelt in an
old house in Old Hurlingham Street, with old link
extinguishers at the door; old windows, with panes
of green glass that spoke of old makers, with the

boss in the middle of the sheet ; an old door, massive enough to have been a teaser to Gordonites and Chartists, but a brand-new door-plate in shining brass with the red lettering, " Blandford, Agent." Franklin's hatter's sign was no more simple in the end.

Mrs. Pleasanton was shown into what had been the dining-room—the house faced the east, so that all the larger fine rooms were at the back, towards the afternoon sun—fitted up as a species of Chesterfield cabinet. A sweet odour lingered in it, as if one of those ladies who will have over every new product of the Boulevard des Capucines, had lately paid a call. There were two alabaster vases, breast high, full of fresh flowers. Above a harmonium, richly inlaid with ivory, hung a copy of Allori's " Car of Fortune pursued by Mankind." On another panel was seen, in an Oxford frame, a steel-plate of old Rothschild. Several rows of shelves were filled with hundreds of knick-knacks, presents apparently, and mineral speci-mens, chiefly of gold-bearing quartz. A model, in native silver, of an American locomotive and a Pullman-car train stood on a tea-table in the middle of the room. The furniture suggested, by the variety of woods, that each article was a sample of the material and of its suitability for the cabinet-makers. In portfolios, held in frames with patent contrivances for relieving the amateur of all trouble while viewing the contents, were plans, drawings, designs, plates of the novelties in ocean steamers, saloon vessels, trains for submarine tunnels, and minor inventions.

In short, Mr. Owen Blandford was the latest outcome of the times. He made a parade of a lack of antecedents, and avowed that nothing would give him more pleasure than to be wedded to a friendless orphan, so as to be unfettered by pledges to society. How could he carry out international schemes, he said, if he were liable to be telegraphed back from Trieste, when he might be knee-deep in a grain speculation; couriered home from Palestine, where he might be planting a Russo-Hebraic colony; worried down a Colorado mine shaft, because an uncle, a father-in-law, or his wife's sister were stricken with measles or hay-fever? Pooh! pooh! Nevertheless, he was pretty well anchored to London.

No one pretended he was an authority on any speciality, but he had run up a fairly substantial scaffolding for future building; and, as in the case of London statues and their preparatory stages, the latter are very often finer works of art and more pleasing to the æsthete than the monstrosity revealed when rope and spar are cleared away.

Blandford was a man of sense and wit, who adapted everything to the precept, " Money makes the Man; " and in order to be such a money maker, he had cast about for a comprehensive craft. He decided to be an agent, a Figaro here and there, leading people by the nose, like the

barber. He was as ready for emergencies as a
conjuror. He began business in a fourth floor in
Cheapside, but came west in a couple of years
with a strong private connection. There are
several solicitors of the old school in Old Hurlingham Street, and very deeply shocked they were
when it oozed out that Blandford had executed
legal manœuvres for some of their best clients,
without any one knowing where he gained the
knowledge of those tricks of fence supposed to
belong to the profession only. They even sought
to rake up one of those cinders that most men
have, after the fires of their youth have waned,
in order to revive a coal; but, as Carpe (who was
legal adviser to several American belles obtaining
English titles) commented : " They wouldn't blaze
up ' worth a cent.' " That appeared to settle for
ever the insinuations that Blandford had mis-
behaved himself, from a police-magistrate's point of
view, twenty years ago. And Owen improved so
rapidly! it was the facility of absorption and
reproducing which the French actress possesses.
He was only passable when he set up at the
back of the Burlington Arcade; yet, in a few
years, he was worthy the Augustan (Lumleian)
Age, presenting the charm of an exquisite edu
cation, polished talent, and refined grace. He
understood how to flavour business with
gossip, company reports with wit, life-and-death
counsel with Voltairian pleasantries. He could

G

interest an iceberg; he knew the right chords to
touch, even in the heartless; could soothe the
lover, and smooth down the irritated. His voice
grew musical, and yet remained manly; his language Orientally flowery when a trustee wavered
on the edge of the abyss of thirty per cent. He
recited an early and unpublished Bab-ble of
Gilbert; hummed you something you had never
heard of Planquette's; meant "Le Bois" of Boulogne,
when he used that abbreviation; threw no cloak
over his Saturday to Monday trip to see the Paris
Sunday races; could water absinthe correctly
as a Zouave, and knew whether Dickey Byrde
was married, and when she first came out in the
T.R., Dory Island. Now and then the newest
fashionable phrases, the very latest turns in the
Prince's set, slipped into his monetary consulta-
tions, like the caricatures of a Don, which by
misadventure fall out of a collegian's atlas when
an ignorant or malicious fellow hands the lam-
pooned Busby the book. For a long while the
general public never suspected Owen Blandford's
importance; but a glimpse, nay, more than that,
was afforded by his first appearance in the police-
court as a prosecutor as well as the accused, a
début signalized by a popular success, amounting
to an ovation of good eggs!

The facts were simple. A lady of title, noted
for charity, had been misled by a fanatic into
reducing her estate quite as much as her husband

might have done if he had been a turfite. He remonstrated, and adopted some means of tightening
the rings on the purse. Mr. Fanatic was cute
and persevering, and suggested ways and means to
juggle the cash away. My lord forbade him the
house. My lady then consulted Mr. Blandford;
at the same time her husband also asked his
advice. Blandford was between the two stools,
but did not fall; on the contrary, it was the
fanatic that fell. He had the impudence, the
agent termed it, to call on him and propose, in
fine, that they two should *exploit* the couple.
Blandford, to his amazement—it is regrettable we
are obliged to repeat this blemish upon our hero
for a chapter—assumed the fiery, revolted tone,
and one word not only led to another, but
Fanatic's hand to the ruler, which bruised the
cheek-bone of the agent. He promptly knocked
his assailant down with a project for " Felling
Mahogany Trees without the Use of the Saw,"
and kicked him out, and across Old Hurlingham
Street into the bootmaker's opposite. And the
kickee had the folly to lodge a complaint against
Mr. Blandford. Blandford defended himself quite
as vigorously as in the combat of arms ; and, what
is more to the point, quite as astutely under the
toga as the priest's counsel. He "kept the lady
out of the case" so dexterously, that, if any one had
proposed it, the gallantry of the Englishman must
have awarded him a golden wreath. The devout

beggar sank away into some remote mission ; the
divided pair were seen at a most frivolous bazaar,
where my lady sold the Japanese delicacy, " hokai-
pokai," at half a sovereign a platter, and my lord
presided over the figure-in-the-flat, which swallows
balls—a convincing proof of a perfect reconciliation; and Mr. Blandford was still more eminent in
his mediatory profession.

Around him was a constant turmoil of proud
names, ponderous fortunes, fair faces—though, in
strict fact, one must record that most of the faces
were rather hooked in nasal projection ; and
recherché carriage-dresses. Mothers consulted
him about bringing out their daughters, since no
one knew so well when Plutus and Patricio would
be in town ; and daughters timidly sought his
advice how to shake off the overgrown boy at Dr.
Reimer's school, with whom they sillily imagined
they were entangled. That power which affects
everything—Fashion—lifted him up, and bore him
still upwards. Sorrow and despair came to him,
and he relieved them by bringing back the runa-
away sons—but not the artful decoy ; the flighty
husband, smitten with one of those gipsy fits
which attack the hitherto abnormally sedate man
of business. On the other hand, there was no
doubt that he laid down the route, profoundly
baffling, for the gigantic defaulter. He answered
a detective who, angry at a wild-goose chase to
Loffoden in the close of autumn, reproached him

bitterly, that he defied him to prove his complicity, and that, after all, he only attended to affairs in which money was involved. One drop of blood and he repelled any contract.

This ever-widening reputation, this intimate knowledge of the uppermost stratum, this familiarity with numberless secrets, so many confidences, such constant intercourse with the highest personages—all the influences, in short, which can be accumulated by an acute, discreet, and pliant go-between, had invested Mr. Owen Blandford with almost unlimited power. Moreover, he wisely joined no political party, and went to church neither more nor less than the established standard of good society requires.

Mrs. Pleasanton stood before the man—so much the average-looking gentleman of semi-legal, semi-financial, and semi-Semitical shaping, that but for a very solid bullet-head, and a rather thick neck, no physiognomist would have accounted him worthy a second glance. His gift was that his organs were, phrenologically speaking, evenly balanced, but probably cunning, greed, and self-esteem, were somewhat in excess.

" Whom have I the honour—? " began the agent, who seemed to be trying to recollect a name.

" Mrs. Colonel Pleasanton, the mother of Mrs. Pryse-Price."

"Certainly. I must beg pardon, Madam ; you are not one easily to be forgotten. But, pray be seated."

Sitting down opposite her, with his back to the light, which is the A of the feline business-man's alphabet, he continued—

"Your daughter's marriage with Mr. Pryse-Price, which has given me the pleasure of your acquaintance, has always been a source of great satisfaction to me, I declare. You and I, Madam, your maternal devotion principally, of course, and I, with my knowledge of financial lights, have effected a truly blissful marriage. Mrs. Pryse-Price chose me to invest her settlement, so handsome a one, and is perfectly satisfied with my suggestion. Her husband is an excellent fellow, sharing what is so rare nowadays—the commendable if somewhat strict sentiments of his wife. After business hours one may pass an evening with pleasure in such remarkably happy households; and I am quite sure that you have not come from any anxiety about that predestined couple."

For a man who was quite certain of a subject, the nervous tremor in his well-schooled voice was contradictory

"Oh, dear, no; that's true. I am very content in that quarter, dear Mr. Blandford. I came on a personal matter."

He fixed his eyes on her, like a botanist who unexpectedly sees a plant throwing out a leaf which threatens a revelation that he had mistaken its true place in creation.

"Oh, Mr. Blandford, years bring about great changes. Up to my age women are diverted with a thousand things : there is the world and society in which to be entertained. We are dazzled, we love the glitter, believe in it as solid, trust in its glamour as not evanescent. We imagine that we shall never feel the want of anything brighter. But, Mr. Blandford, I have arrived at the barrier beyond which I see fresher, purer views. You understand me, I dare say. I feel the emptiness of my life. Nothing interests me. I wish to return to the quiet country life in which I was bred. I know how wise is your counsel, what strength there is in your guiding hand, to help me back to rustic tranquillity."

Whilst speaking with much volubility the lady's eyes, which avoided those of her hearer, as if she felt them too piercing, had mechanically fallen on something which glittered on the table : a jewel-case partly opened.

"Oh, this box," said the agent, catching the glance, and replying to her thoughts—not to her words—"this surprises you in an office. It is a suite of diamonds. Oh, you may look ! and feast your sight, for they are very fine ones—Old Brazils, not Capes." He handed her the jewels. "It is usually in the rough that I have precious stones here ; but this is not a diamond dealer's. You may have seen the owner depart as you came in. No ? Oh, she had her veil down, and only by her carriage could you have recognised her. Rather notorious, I assure you ; daughter of a Lea River gardener, but wedded of late years, for her beauty, of a most aristocratic type, to an eminent nobleman. She tells me that she has gone through the most incredible persecutions to arrive at this reward; rejected bountiful offers to take to the stage ; starved rather than be an artist's model, and I do not know what that beauty in poverty was subjected to. Now she is rich, that is, she is surrounded by wealth, but has no control of the purse, and to obtain a large sum she must raise money on this set of jewels, which will not be missed, she hopes, till redeemed. She seeks my aid to find a child, the offspring of an unfortunate sister, dead when the two were in poverty together, whom she allowed to be adopted by strangers."

Mrs. Pleasanton sighed, and almost glared, her eyes were so distended with growing attention. Such hunger to recover the boy who was taken away before the mother even saw it, is startling —she could not be more sympathetic if it were her own child.

Mrs. Pleasanton was as white as a ghost; but the speaker, who took careful heed not to notice her agitation, betrayed, to a cooler head, that he was essaying a trial of her fortitude under an unexpected shock.

" But how wrong I am to repeat such stories,

even if I am impressed with them, and require
the relief of a sympathetic confidante! There,
there," closing the case with a snap. "Let me see.
Have you not another daughter nearly of a marriageable age?—an extremely lively child, quite a
peculiar disposition. Is she married too, by this
time?"

"Not yet, Mr. Blandford," was the rejoinder
of the lady, far from calm again, but recovering
some colour with the change in the conversation;
"and that is a great source of uneasiness for me.
No one can form an idea of her obstinacy; quite
the antipodes of her sister in disposition. She has
one of those tempers most trying to a mother. I
would much rather she had a little less mind. We
have found most desirable suitors for her; but
she refuses them one after another. Her father
spoils her so. Last evening—"

"The father's pet. I see. What a pity! I
should have thought your boy *jam satis*, ha! ha!
hem;" he brought himself up with the cough. "A
fine active gentleman who aims high for a partner,
I fancy."

" Of course you have met him, Mr. Blandford?"

" I had that pleasure once, at his sister's, when
I went to see her about her investments. But I
have good accounts of him from every quarter.
You are a fortunate mother, Mrs. Pleasanton."

But as his hand, in a sort of complimentary
tapping on the table, rapped the jewel-case of

which the story had excited his visitor's unaccount-
able terror, the effect of the compliment was
annulled by her convulsive start and a return of
her pallor.

" You are very kind to repeat this to please me,
sir.   What a loss that you are not acquaintances,
so that you could be interested in his progress.   J
am sure he would do well as secretary to one of
those great companies you engineer so grandly.
My son must know you and serve you.   You can
do so much."

The agent shook his head with dissent, wherein
mock modesty and affected melancholy were
mingled.   " No, Madam, you flatter us.   I am
not even a promoter.   We formers of companies
are far from what the public say.   We sometimes
succeed in doing a whole nation good, but with
how many unsuccessful projects is the victorious
edifice built ! If you only knew how insignificant
any one man is in these days of association. People
dread the monopolist's influence, they shun him as
a pariah, and do not wish to meet him out of
'Change, or to speak to him out of his own residence.   Your son will thrive better without my
humble hand.   If he has money he can accumu-
late secretaryships—it is a mere question of investment.   I could put him into the Trans-
Andesian Tunnel to-morrow, but they want three
thousand for newspaper charges before they will
look at his testimonials."

Mrs. Pleasanton was merely tickled by the feeler, and smiled a confident smile. So he opened the fire after all this skirmishing with unmasked audacity, saying:

" My dear Mrs. Pleasanton, however much money a young gentleman has to dispose of, he will always wish he had more; and it is painful for youthful financiers to be in that fix. I know the torture by heart. Why not marry him to some rich *parti?* Of course you never thought of that. One does for the girls, but the boy is let over-turn himself on his bicycle at the gate of some suburban villa, to be nursed by the young lady, and, upon convalescence, to recompense her with his hand. This is our modern version of the old romantic episode. Thus is he wasted—I am speaking sordidly—when he might have doubled his income at the trouble of donning a wedding suit, and the cost of half-a-dozen lockets to the bride's cousins."

" But, Mr. Blandford, where are such valuable alliances to be found ? My son indeed aims high."

" Why, I could run off on my fingers the names of—you smile ! you put me on my mettle ! I'll make you look serious before you leave my office !" Here he opened a drawer with a spring-lock, and took out a small book in which was a species of shorthand, perhaps also in a foreign tongue, for he had to puzzle it out slowly. Then he recited these entries : " Twenty-five thousand pounds in consols, and in sound bonds. Ten thousand clear on the wedding-day. No father or mother. Fifty-four thousand on the death of uncles and aunts, unmarried, and who will never marry. Nineteen, ladylike, prettier than her maid tells her."

"It falls below his mark," said the proud mother, though with glittering eyes.

"Stay!" here he turned the leaves backwards rapidly, and stopped in the beginning where the first three letters of the alphabet might be expected to be if the book was so arranged. "I have it, and neighbours too. Is not that providential?"

He wrote a name on his porcelain tablet in the shape of a horseshoe, and tilted it to catch the light and her visual rays. She nodded.

"Yes, we know the Millwards already. But is he so rich—"

"I can only give the figure approximately, Madam, as yet. But you need not fear for your son if he can make an impression there."

"He has already paid some attention to Miss Cicely Millward, but—"

"That's where he made a mistake; but no one can blame him. I have it ticked off here as important that it is not to the elder sister, but to the younger that Mr. M. will leave the bulk of his property."

"Why, sir, such a hint is worth—"

" My dear Madam, your son and I can regulate the business part of the affair. I really detest talking money to ladies. It is understood, then : Mr. Henry Pleasanton lays siege, as I suppose his military father would say, to Miss—" he glanced at his private register—" Naomi Millward! A Jewish name, but though I have been taken for one of 'the good people,' I do not know the meaning. By the way, if the project shapes out nicely, I expect to have the pleasure of seeing you again—"

" It will be my pleasure—"

" Upon which occasion, you could bring that daughter whom you have mentioned as a nettle among the roses."

There was a flutter in his voice, perceptible to maternal ears, for Mrs. Pleasanton was about to dart an inquisitive look upon the agent, but, on the slight turn, she saw the jewel-case, and governed her impulse. On his part, Blandford felt that he had said too much or too little, and to cover the cause for suspicion, if so slight a thing could have excited it, he added, as he retreated a step and threw open a door to unveil a vista of a couple of trees, a waterless fountain in blue-grey marble, and a grass-plot beyond the intervening room:

" I can only offer you a luncheon here, but I have my cooking done at the Paratonnerre Hotel adjacent—something *soigné*—and—naturally, your

son will make one of the party." This suggestion
made the coming of Marcia possible, and Mrs.
Pleasanton gave a promise, and was escorted to the
street-door by the agent while pouring out her
thanks. The porter assumed her to be a countess
at the least, at this unusual attention. His master,
retiring into the inner apartment, broke up a
macaroon into the aquarium in a dark corner,
where the golden carp but dully gleamed, and
muttered—

"So, Harry Pleasanton is my rival with Cicely.
I fancy I have spiked his gun bearing upon her."
Then, remembering the jewel-case which he had
left incautiously on the table, he darted in upon
it with the alacrity of a man of twenty-five, and
locked it up in a safe. "There's a profitable
skeleton in that house," he added, "the house of
Pleasanton; and if that girl has grown up into
anything like the image I now picture of her, I
shall 'make no bones' of becoming a factor in her
fortunes too."

Whereupon Mr. Meddlewithall, as a Jonsonian
dramatist might have designated him, drank a
very little brandy in some mineral water with the
moderation of a man whose head is the cannon-
ball with which, according to Balzac, one must
cleave the crowd to hit the target of fortune.

CHAPTER IX.

HENRY PLEASANTON, like many another of the present day, did not tell his age according to his years, but according to the time he had lived among men. The coldness of our youth—a peculiar characteristic of the second half of the nineteenth century—was seen in all his actions. He looked serious, and seemed to be calculating. In him were to be recognised those contrary elements of the plutocratic temperament, which, in our social history, constitutes groups without fusion, and parties without leaders.

He had been of that class of children whom nothing astonishes and nothing amuses, who, when taken to the pantomime, look on without excitement, and repeat no pranks of the clown next day, nor even snub their sister as less pretty than Columbine. Even in his early childhood he was wary and thoughtful. When at school he was never found dreaming of the future, never regarding pure vacancy, but contemplating some sparkling object in the void. He experienced none of those vague temptations, saw none of those vivid visions which fill the imaginations of sixteen with agitations of delight. There were two or three sons of political celebrities in his class, and with these he instinctively associated. Even at college he thought of the London club he would join.

After leaving his *alma mater*, Henry lived steadily, and his bachelor life was a quiet one. He was not to be seen where young men brushed off their effervescence, and billiard, roulette, dancing *balls*, were equally ignored. He rode a quieter horse than his groom, played whist, and avowed ignorance of " Nap," and shunned military men and those sun-blacked travellers who could not understand the shudder of their auditors when it leaked out in their narrative that those hands of theirs had pulled the trigger at the head of a slave hunter disputing their explorative path. He spent his evenings in the somewhat forgotten drawing-rooms of those mysterious old dames who dwell in Russell Square (even there princes call to see them, to the bewilderment of their coach-men and the neighbourhood), Clapham way, and up North, and courted the society of the decidedly *passée*. It is true that what would have told against him elsewhere, served him among frumps and faded belles. His coldness was deemed charming gravity, his premature seriousness had a kind of fascination. There are fashions for manly graces. The Victorian reign, with its large universal fortunes, had accustomed the great political reception rooms to prize in a man of fashion what we may call that shadow of the silk gown, which the Q.C. and Professor always carry about them into the world, even after they become notabilities. To a taste for wit, for lively, gay, broadly dazzling qualities, which Kings George and William had preferred, succeeded amongst the women of the upper middle classes a taste for conversation in the lecture vein, for the science of the professor's chair, for a sort of pedantic amiability. The pedant did not terrify, even when old; when young, he could scarcely fail to please; and the report spread that Henry Pleasanton bewitched the dames who played with Amazonian bows and regretted that Miss Bloomer had come over here, like "Tramway Train," twenty years too soon.

He was of a practical turn of mind. He professed the worship of the useful, mathematical truths, positive religions, and all the exact sciences. He could not quote Comte, but he cited his English disciples. He knew Emerson by correspondence, and had an autograph poem from Walt Whitman. He tolerated Art, and maintained that Buhl ornaments had never been better made than by John Bull. Political Economy having appeared to him, on his entering the world, a vocation as well as a career, he had resolutely become an

H

economist, and wrote it *œconomist* to attract attention. He had applied to this dry study a limited but patient and diligent intellect, and his name came out in the great Reviews, attached to some heavy article, crammed with figures, which the novel-reading women skipped, and the men " put under the table as read" along with the advertisements at the back.

From the interest which it professes for the lower classes, as its principal foraging ground from its being occupied with their welfare, and from the algebraical record which it keeps of their sufferings, Political Economy had naturally imparted to Henry Pleasanton a tinge of Liberalism. Not that he was very decidedly in the Liberal ranks; for he wished to hedge, to be in the position of that dark feature in former American politics, "the nigger in the farce." His opinions jutted but slightly in advance of the old Whig principles, amongst that crowd of convictions which anticipate the future, pave the way for their adoption, and make certain what might possibly have happened. His war against power was limited to a stroke of satire, a covert allusion, the meaning and the key of which his toadies explained to any one lenient to bores. In fact, he rather coquetted with, than was hostile to the Government *pro tem.* The connections he formed, and the society into which he was thrown, kept him within reach of Government influence, and on the skirts of

Government patronage ; but no post lucrative enough had offered itself : he required a wet blanket, not a twopenny extinguisher. He prepared the works and corrected the orations for a noble sinecurist who had scarcely time even to subscribe his name to his books. He excelled in those double dealings, compromises, " arrangements," which kept him on confidential terms with all parties, and made the path of promotion easy.

This great little man's mother beamed at her son's servant when she called at his lodgings, after her interview with Mr. Blandford. As she passed in, she smiled at the apartment, the ornaments, and the furniture, and through the window at the Turkestan Envoy's residence over the way.

She entered Henry's study, where he was writing ; no cigarette, no curaçao, no theatre tickets, nothing of that sort beside his inkstand.

" So you have followed me close ! " cried he, leaning back in the arm-chair to let his mother kiss him : and then, flourishing his porcupine quill nervously, he went on : " Why, you never breathed a syllable last night. What has brought you ? "

" Oh, shopping, formal visits. You know I always put off things till the last moment, and when I do come to London, dash them off in a bunch. How comfortable you are here ! "

"Oh, yes ; the sun comes in nicely, for the street is one of the widest in London. You have not seen these new apartments, I remember now."

"How well you manage—there is no one like you ! You are quite sure about the drains ?"

Pleasanton laughed.

"We only fear the quarterly drain of rent and taxes."

" Your curtains are very thick, and there's no fan in the upper panes. Be sure you tell your servant to air the room well every time you go out, won't you ?"

"I'll make a note of it," answered the young man, in the careless tone in which we answer a child.

"Oh, why have you those things ; I don't like them ?" She had just caught sight of a trophy of arms, over a bookcase. "The sight of them is enough! I very soon had your papa's sword put away in his study, where no one goes."

"The pistols are not loaded. Besides, what with burglars by night, and those fellows of the Volunteer Horse Marines—I beg their pardon, the Volunteer Privateers—worrying one to join by day, I have gone in for fencing and shooting— one meets some very desirable acquaintance at Captain Desdichado's. The acquirement of the arts of self-defence renders one calm when a bully threatens to injure the human face divine."

Mrs. Pleasanton shut her eyes for an instant after sitting down. "You don't know how this horrid bachelor's life of yours makes me tremble, Henry," she sighed. "If you were married, I am sure I should not be so fretful. How I should like to see you in a home of your own, Henry."

"So should I, I assure you, mother!"

"Is that the truth? You know that no secrets should be kept from a mother! I am afraid, though, a handsome bachelor like you, so accomplished and fascinating, may have more than one reason for not wedding."

Henry burst out laughing, at the idea of a woman enchaining such a chameleon as he.

"Ah, my dear mother, rest assured if I had an attachment, it would be one easy to snap! I have no time to cab about matching beads and replacing broken fans."

"Well, then, how came you to miss the match with Miss Calhoun? It was you that spoilt it all."

"Miss Calhoun! Father made me acquainted with the Calhoun principal at his wine merchant's, I remember. It was an ambuscade into which you sent me, without a cartridge of caution! You certainly are very unwise, mother. I was announced by a servant with potato peels in his mouth, as 'Master Plisantune!' as if I were a boy or a legal dignitary, with a wink to the other footmen as much as to say, 'Here comes on-

little darlint's intended, sure!' I find the mistress of the house, whom I had seen twice, and
no more, rushing at me to overwhelm me with
smiles ; her son, whom I did not know at all,
shakes hands with me, till every knuckle
cracks. In the room there is also a tall figure
with red hair, a marvellous complexion, I grant
you, but with freckles and high cheek-bones.
Well, of course I am placed next this young lady
at dinner. Hers was a good old family, property realisable, tastes simple. Not a word from
her till something put that of Carlow in her
mouth, and then she was fluent ; and I thought
she meant a favourite pug all the while. 'So
you love it,' said I. 'I wish I may doy beside it!'
says she ; and poor guileless me, that thought the
brogue a fiction out of books. 'Och !' I said—this
was to float with the stream—'och, happy the
dog's death beside you !' and then it came out
the tale was a very different caudal appendage
altogether. If they had money it was kept in a
stocking, worsted home-knit at that! Pray
plan no further matrimonial plots on my behalf."

"You shall see how I fall to work wife-hunting."

" Make your mind easy, ma ; I am not one of
those who are caught with 'Fair, fair, with
auricomus hair!' and 'So kind to the loved
ones at home !' You see, I have reflected a good
deal on marriage, though you might not think so.
The most difficult and costly prize to acquire in

this world is money, you'll admit. One seeks but the happiness and the honour of being rich, the respect and consideration attending King Midas. Well, the wise fortune-seeker's means of obtaining this money, directly and immediately, without fatigue, pain, or genius, simply, naturally and honourably, as the world goes, is by marriage. I have discovered, besides, that to make a rich alliance there is no need to be wondrously handsome, nor amazingly captivating : it is merely necessary to determine on coolly, and with all your strength, staking your chances on the single card. Lastly, I have seen that, in playing this game of all 'on the turn,' it is quite as easy to pull off an extraordinary stake as an ordinary one, to marry gold as copper : it all depends on selecting the big bank. The play is the same. Do not waste your time with these landowners who cannot get in their rents, these noblemen whose castles are not worth renovating, these wholesale teamen who cannot compete with the scientific adulterator, whose willow leaves undersell him without any Suez Canal charges ! I'll take the sister of the tenor who has made a fortune in five years ; the niece of the theatrical manager who has run a spectacular melodrama five hundred nights ; the daughter of a *fence*—if he has been clever enough to hang his customers and hoodwink the police !— only let the money be secure. And now do you pardon me for my candour ? "

His auditress was struck dumb with astonishment at such cynical frankness, but admiration succeeded. Seeing this, he concluded : "Don't fret yourself, therefore, dear mother! I shall marry gold—and perhaps sooner than you hope."

"But I have already paved the way," she managed to falter, and gave him an account of her conference with Mr. Blandford.

Henry listened with his underlip drawn in with a species of apprehension. Blandford was one of the few men whom he dreaded to "tackle."

"Millward! The elder daughter not his heiress ? " he repeated.

"No one ever knew Mr. Blandford to be misinformed."

"It is true Cicely is not his favourite. This must be attended to."

"I thought so. But not a word to your father."

"No, no, the Gordian knot of marriage is to be tied, not severed. But, if you please, mother dear, as the *Revue Economique* goes to press on the twenty-second, and I am a slow hand at writing in French, you might let me finish this paper— 'The trajectory of Humanity is a spiral curve, not a circle'—and I'll run down to morrow afternoon."

She left him proud and satisfied ; but the moment he was alone, Henry flung down the pen with a spatter so contrary to his neatness-loving disposition, that it was a memorable trait, and growled with a knitting of his gummed eyebrows:

"If I make love to Naomi, what the deuce and all in the way of a tigress's cruelty will not Cicely do?"

CHAPTER X.

"NOT late!" exclaimed Marcia, breathless after a run down the stairs and a bound into the breakfast-room at eleven; "I thought every one had come down. Where is mamma?"

"Gone to town, Marsie, to make some calls," replied her father.

"Ah! has not Mr. Reudall come over?"

"He looked in, would not stay for coffee, and is at the Works. He says the stuff he is experimenting must combine or blow up. I am loth to have him shot up our chimney into the moon. Well, come to breakfast, child."

But, instead of sitting down, Marcia ran to her father, wound her arms round his neck, and began kissing and hugging him like a white bear seizing a walrus.

"There, there, that will do, wild catamountain," groaned the old soldier, smiling as he struggled with her.

"Let me give you one pinching kiss, so!"—she nipped up his cheeks between the thumb and

index finger on either side, and altered the shape
of his mouth as if his face were india-rubber.

" What an irrepressible torment you are ! "

" Look at me ; let me see if a little Marcia is in
your eyes ! ope your e'en, auld Colin Campbell
that you are ! " and rising after another kiss, she
held her father's head in her flattened hands, and
held it at arms' length as if detached from his
body, after the precedent of Medusa's, the shield of
Perseus. They thus looked into each others' eyes,
as if souls dwelt in the profundities.

The glass door of the breakfast-room was open,
letting in the auroral brightness, and the perfumes
and sounds from the garden ; one sunbeam, which
fell on the table, shone on the china and sparkled
in the glasses. A gentle breeze fanned the leaves
so that their shadows formed a trembling pattern on the floor, as if the crumb-cloth were
the chalking board of a lace-designer. From the
distance came a vague murmur of the wings of
birds chasing the flies among the flowers.

" A *tête-à-tête*, is it not ? What is the new word
that supersedes jolly ? " asked Marcia, twisting up
her nose as the coffee-pot steamed up to take
the starch out of her frills. " The table is altogether too large for two ; I am too far off. I
feel like Crusoe on his island ! " Taking up her
plate and " accessories," she seated herself close by
her father's side, like the last comer at an ordinary,
for whom a couple have grudgingly made room.

"As I have my papa all to myself to-day, I mean to enjoy his company thoroughly!" And she edged up again, as a raw recruit leans towards the grizzled comrade for a reassuring nudge of the elbow.

"Ah! now you remind me of the time when you would always play at meals with me—but you were only eight years old or so then."

Marcia laughed. "Funny little girl, wasn't I?"

"I was in for a wigging, last night," resumed the colonel, after a moment's silence, as he laid down his knife and fork.

"Don't say so!" cried Marcia, quietly trapping a fly in the sugar-bowl, and then lifting the lid just a wee bit to let him come out in a trepidation. "Did you have a happy release, like Blue Bottle? Poor old papa! Why, what did you do to merit a 'wigging'?"

"You are the last one that should ask. You know wherefore better than I, you family lightning-rod! You bring all the thunder down upon me!"

"Oh! if you tie me up to the halberds, colonel, I'll pretend I want to whisper my confession, and kiss you!" And so saying she began to unfold her tall figure in a skyward direction.

"Sit down, girl!" the other said, in a tone which he tried to imbue with pretended severity. "My dear one, you must admit that last evening—"

"Oh, papa! is that the way you talk to me on such a soft, sweet day? it is out of all keeping!"

"But," went on the censor, endeavouring to preserve a dignified demeanour towards the rebellious airs of his daughter, in which contrition and defiance were equally mingled, "will you explain to me? for you evidently acted so in malice aforethought."

Marcia gave two or three sharp, emphatic nods, as she blinked mischievously.

"I am speaking seriously to you, Marcia."

"So am I serious, very—one of a serious family. Mamma has already told me that I did what I have done on purpose."

"I should like to know why?"

"I will reveal the dread secret on condition that it does not make you too conceited. It is all because—"

"Out with it! or no more tea!"

"Because I love you much better than any body in the world, away and beyond Mr. Goddard —there!"

"But, then, people ought not to be asked here if you are going to wrap yourself up in the paternal love-proof. If you had not liked the young man, why have him here? We did not try to force your inclinations. It was you who allowed matters to go so far. Your mother and I even thought that Mr. Goddard pleased—"

"Pardon me, papa; if I had refused to see

Mr. Goddard a second time, you would have said I was hasty, mad, thoughtless. At least that is the way mamma would talk. Instead of this, mind, what have I done that you can blame me for? I have seen the gentleman again and again, and have taken time to form my opinion. I am thoroughly convinced of an antipathy which is perhaps very silly, but which exists."

"But why not have told us? We would have found many ways of getting rid of him."

"You are ungrateful, papa. I have saved you that annoyance. The young gentleman retires, though anything but a retiring young man; tiring, not retiring—I will have my puns!—and you have nothing to do with it. The entire transaction is mine own act. And see the thanks I get for my self-devotion! Another time, you shall meet the onset without me in the vanguard."

"Listen to me, dear one. If I speak gravely to you, it is because your future is in question, your marriage! I have been a long time trying to accustom myself to the idea of separation. Fathers can be selfish too, you see: they would wish a dear daughter never to leave them. It is so difficult to imagine her happy unless they saw her daily smile. But a man must be reasonable, and let things go on in the world according to ancient regulations. At length it seems to me that I could love a son-in-law. It is because I am getting old, my dear little woman." Pleasanton took both his daughter's hands in his single grasp. "Your father is sixty-eight, my child, and worn with wild, savage battles. I have barely time to see you beginning to be happy. It is my hourly thought. Your mother also loves you, I know, but between her character and yours there is a wide difference; and if I were to be taken away! Don't flinch, be a soldier's daughter! we must reflect on these things, and, at my age, deeply too. You see the idea of leaving you without a protector, without some passion which would replace in your heart the affection for your old father—"

The veteran could not proceed. His daughter embraced him, choking with sobs, and wept on his breast.

"How cruel you are!" sobbed she; "why do you speak of ghastly things? Never, never!" and with a gesture she repulsed the black care which was evidently darkening the noon-light with its raven wings.

The colonel had rested her against his knee. He pressed her in his arms, kissed her forehead, and begged her to compose herself.

She again repeated: "Never, oh, cruel one!" as if she was struggling with some horrid dream. At last drying her eyes, she managed to falter, "Let me go and have a good cry by myself," and fled away, groping with tear-blinded eyes.

"Mr. Varney is certainly daft," observed Mr. Rendall, as he entered—luckily by the verandah and window—"I have just now been able to tear myself away from him. Alone, sir?"

"Yes, my wife ran up to town. Marcia has just gone out the room. You two are like the weather couple on a post at Elmwood, one out t'other goes in."

"But how badly you look, colonel!"

"I? Not at all; I have just had a little vexation about Marcia and her marriage; about Mr. Goddard. I have been silly enough to tell her that I was anxious to see her with a life guardian; that fathers of my age are not immortal, and all that strain. Whereupon—the poor child is so easily affected, you know—she went off crying to her room. * She must have time to recover. Meanwhile I shall look after the Works, and expect you there."

Rendall took a cup of coffee, found the *Post*, and went into the garden to read. He had been there fully half-an-hour, when he saw Marcia approaching. She had her hat on, and her animated countenance shone full of joy, in serene and tender enthusiasm.

"Where do you drop from?"

"From heaven, I hope," replied Marcia, "*viâ* the cottage of old Fordice; his leg is much better, and he is going out with two sticks. So patient under the pain; so hopeful and reliant on the

God of the Poor Man, as he says, that I am not irreverent in deeming his cottage one of the ante-chambers of the eternal mansion. It has made me cry terribly! I wonder my hat-bow is not spotted as if I had been caught in a shower." She "shot" her arms forward in a sweeping movement, that pretty trick since tight sleeves fettered woman, in order to untie the knot mentioned. "When he had limped away, I looked at his Bible, and seeing the text—you will not let me try the *sortes*, when you are by, but it does come apt sometimes—I read, oh, Mr. Rendall, I read: 'Because thine heart was tender, and thou didst humble thyself, behold, I will gather thee to thy fathers, and thou shalt be gathered to their grave in peace!' And down I fell upon my stubborn knees, Carroll, and prayed that I might die before papa, if not at the same moment."

"Die!" interrupted Rendall, springing up and casting away the journal, like a warrior who hears a trumpet challenge, and stares before him for an enemy.

"And since then I have been repeating the lines like music. It is balm to my heart to feel as if my prayer would be answered!"

She went on her way to the house, with her bared head gleaming, and her face irradiated.

"Poor girl!" muttered Rendall. "That woman wants to get her out of the house, so as to worry the old man into the grave, and bestow his money wholly on that icicle of a son! By all that's sacred, if he were not her brother I'd thrash him as soundly as Goddard and all the rest of her persecutors!"

CHAPTER XI.

CARROLL'S COMRADES.

A FEW days later the Pleasantons and Mr. Rendall were seated together in the garden behind the house. The largest tree in the garden was an American tulip-pine, rejoicing in an aggressive independence characteristic of its origin, which led to its times of flowering being quite a moot question. Rose trees were trained amongst its lower limbs, and its green branches were clustered with wisteria flowers. Under the tree was a swing; behind it shrubberies of lilacs and brambles; in front a grass-plot, a seat, and a fountain bordered with white shells. The jet had never played within the memory of man; it was full of hopeful aquatic plants, nevertheless, and a few newts were plashing about in a very small pool of rain or dew.

"Have you quite given up thinking of the theatricals, Marcia?" inquired young Pleasanton of his sister. "Is the idea altogether abandoned, like your hundred others per week?"

"Not at all, sir! I can't help delays. It is no fault of this child! I would be delighted to

act at any time ; but I can find nobody to co-
operate. Unless I were to come out in a monologue
like Madame Chaumont, when she was down at
the Millward's *soirée*, what can I do ? Mr.
Rendall won't make the red fire ! You are a
serious man," she went on to her brother, " so
what's the use in asking you ? "

" I don't object to private theatricals, and would
play willingly," said the heir.

"You, Henry ! " ejaculated Mrs. Pleasanton,
with astonishment.

" But we are not short of gentlemen," resumed
Marcia. " There are always men to be had. It
is the other column of the 'cast.' I see no ladies
in the neighbourhood."

"Pooh ! " said Henry, "you have not half
looked."

" Oh, haven't I, Mr. Know-all ! "

" Mr. Boxby's daughter. Ay, surely ! why not
Miss Boxby, eh ? They are at Slither's End
now—so convenient for rehearsals. Delia is
rather a simpleton, but I think for the part of
Miss Parbuckle—"

" What ! " blurted out the chemical professor,
"do you still think of doing 'One Fool Makes
Many ? ' "

" Now for a scolding ! Suppose the part I
should take is the heroine so much made love to
—what's the objection if my brother plays in
it ? "

Henry smiled, and Mr. Rendall stared at this poser in moral logic.

"But," he remonstrated, " he might not be on the stage when you are being courted!"

"But we can print his name next to mine in the programme, and strangers will see our relation —that I am under his pinion, don't you see?"

Whether Rendall was convinced or not, he only observed:

"Going to benefit the parish poor?"

"Yes, or build a new wing to something or other somewhere in the country. Buy Fordice a crutch—"

"Not so fast! I mean you are too slow," broke in the colonel.

He had attended to the needs of the man injured in his service.

"They will say, "For the Poor, by *poor* actors, just for a skit!" said Henry

" I don't care a pin what they say, if they pay for their places. They cannot expect Irving and Ristori in Gratchley."

" Well, Delia Boxby, to begin with, mamma. What, do you object to her?"

" They are not of our set, my dear child," quickly replied Mrs. Pleasanton. "They are fresh from the shop; Mr Boxby was the innovator who got a licence to sell spirituous refreshments to his patronesses in a little buffet next the glove counter, that's how he began to make his money!"

Although she was at heart no spiteful woman,
Mrs. Pleasanton seldom let an opportunity pass of
thus depreciating, with expressions of contempt and
superb disdain, the origin of the fortune and position
of every one about whom the Blandford's posted
her up. It was not from malice, nor from the
pleasure of slander, but from sheer envy. She
denied the importance, the respectability, even the
income which was ascribed to people, simply from
the prodigious pride of one a couple of removes
from such a class.

"Inconsistency!" cried the colonel. "Boxby,
you pretend, poisoned his customers, and what do
I do with my confounded chimneys but blast the
vegetation for miles around? at least, I did, till
Rendall came down and exorcised the fumes in
that magical way he subdues everything. You
may as well drop the roster—this wife of mine
can blot out all the other names with more stories
like that about all the people we know!"

"Now, papa, suppose we should have pretty
little Remoli over! you like her!"

"I do, I do. But ask your mother."

"That Remoli girl? But, my dear, don't you
know—"

"I know nothing injurious to her, a sweet
pet!"

"You never heard her father's history? A
wretched Italian stucco-plasterer. He comes to
London without a penny, he buys—though where

he got the money I don't know—a shed and a bit of ground at St. John's Wood, and after grubbing on as an image moulder for the artists thereabouts, the railway came upon him and enriched him."

"Now I'll tell you where he got his courage from to go on toiling till that fluke enriched him," burst in Colonel Pleasanton, like the final charge when the cry goes up at the end of a contested day that "they waver! they fall back!" "He fell like that classic wrestler upon the battle-field, soaked with his comrades' blood, and rose each time refreshed with valour. If a man were to slander his daughter, I'd take him by the ear over to Boulogne sands and run him through under the cliffs."

There was a silence after this energetic outburst.

"Little Remoli,' was accepted in this lull.

"You wander too far afield," remarked young Pleasanton. "Why not include the Misses Millward?" His mother could not help beaming an approval. "They happen to be here his month."

"The Misses Millward!" repeated Mrs. Pleasanton, pleasedly.

"Naomi?" quickly replied Marcia. "I should like her very well indeed. But I noticed a coolness in her sister towards me last winter. Something has set Cicely against me—I don't know what."

"She turned crusty," explained the colonel
with ursine Bismarckian diplomacy, "because she
is the heiress to a great amount. It's the father's
suggestion. Such sires do not wish their daughters
to enjoy the acquaintance of girls who have
brothers turned twenty. She was cautioned to
drop the gingerbread not gilt both sides."

The eyes of Mrs. Pleasanton and her son
flashed fire. There is nothing like a cavalry spur
to catch trains and a cavalry heel to step on gouty
corns.

"I do not see what the Millwards have to be
proud about. One need not look in Debrett to
know what he is descended from."

"D'ye hear my wife?" whispered the veteran to
his chemical adviser; "she will bring him down
a bricklayer's ladder; poor old Millward!"

"Yes, hers is a fearful furnace to pass through,"
muttered Rendall. "I wish she'd invent one for
the Works. It would make phosphor bronze run
like cream in thirty seconds."

"However," continued the social assayer, "they
have always been very polite to you, Henry. Mr.
Millward seemed altogether friendly."

"Not a doubt of it. The last time I met him,
it was in town; he even complained several times
that you do not go over with Marsie, to see his
daughters."

"Indeed?" queried Miss Pleasanton, du-
biously.

"Francis," asked her mother, "what do you think of what Henry says?"

"What objection could I possibly make?"

"Then," said Mrs. Pleasanton, "we shall adopt Henry's idea. We'll go on Saturday. You'll come with us, Henry?"

"I'll go straight there from town."

A few hours after, everyone was at rest, except Marcia who had disinterred a china plate on which she had begun Naomi's portrait; the professor, who was juggling with some powder with all that affecting calmness of the modern Friar Bacon, confident that he will not fire the spoonful of snowy crystals which would demolish the house and excavate a pit to bury a regiment within and Henry—we nearly forgot that important personage—who was walking up and down his room with an extinguished cigar in his mouth. From time to time he seemed to smile, as overcoming some difficulty in his lucubrations.

It was not usual for Marcia to draw or paint in her room, for she had a little studio built out of the remains of the old and too small green-house. It was hidden at the bottom of the garden, rather rustic, ivy-covered and embosomed in foliage, something between a nest and a bower.

On a table covered with an Algerine cloth there lay, this morning, in the miniature studio, a blue-pattern japan ink dish, a lemon, an old print with the de Thou bookmark on its margin, and

two or three other objects of bright colour grouped
in the most natural manner possible for a painting,
under the light which came through the ground
glass roof.   Before the table, on a canvas already
laid in, Marcia was painting with needle-pointed
pencils.   The skirt of her plain grey nun's cloth
dress, fell from under a linen jacket in ample
folds, on each side of the stool revolving, to enable
her to keep level with her work.   Passing through
the garden she had picked a rose, which she placed in
her hair, above one ear, as the pickers for the per-
fumers sometimes wear a very fine specimen in
the south of France.   Her foot, peeping from
under her dress, displayed a little of a fancy
ribbed stocking, as it rested on the front cross-bar
of the easel.

Rendall was near her, watching her at work,
and attempting a drawing of her profile in a
sketch-book he had picked up in a corner, a drawing woefully stiff, as became a man who detested
anything but mathematically true lines in the
straight or round.

"Oh, do sit quietly!" said he, as he pointed
his pencil to give her time to settle down again.
" I would as soon try to catch a sunbeam as your
ikeness.   How can you keep shifting about that
way ?"

"Come now, Carroll! no nonsense with your
portraiture.   I hope you are going to flatter me a
ittle ; and when it comes to the colouring, like

mamma's tirades against the *parvenus*, lay it on thick."

" No more than Dan Phœbus would. I have the conscientiousness of a photographist."

"Let me see it," said she, as she leant back towards him, crossing her maul-stick and palette before her like an Arab salaaming with javelin and shield in his grasp. "I shall not do for a beauty. The Gratchley Geranium will not be the *furore* of the Academy, from the hand of the ancient professor Rendall. Really, now, am I like *that?*"

" A little. Tell me truly, Marcia, what do you think of yourself? Are you handsome?"

" Far from it."

" Pretty? "

" No, no!"

"Ha, ha! you hesitated a little that time."

" Yes, but I said the negative twice."

" Very good. If you don't think yourself handsome nor pretty, I'm sure you don't think yourself —t'other way? Do you?"

No, I do not. It is very difficult to explain to you. Some days, when I look in the glass, I wonder who the face—how can I tell you? In short, I like myself. I don't care to change! It is not my face, I know that well enough. It is an air I wear at such times, something in me, which I feel shines out in my features! Is it the soul speaking in its own silent way? It is some indescribable happiness, vivaciously manifesting itself. There are moments like these when, meseems—there's old English for you! when meseems, I should trick a beholder into a very fair opinion of Miss Pleasanton. You must see me in some such mood, as a treat! Still I should like to have been handsome as a picture, as a statue, but heavens knows in what style! "

"Salvator Rosa!"

"A gipsy! go to, thou scurrilous varlet! more old English! I think I should have liked to be tall, one of those Luca Signorellis, with black hair, and splendid eyes! It's insipid to be between colours! And then the complexion! they rave about the English complexion, but I should like a tawny—no, an orange dash—there, that does it—"illustrating"—a wash of vermilion over chrome, only I cannot show you in oil. Little Remoli's mamma shows it. Then I should stand for hours before my glass—as I do *not* now. I do not know the frame of mine! In the same way when I have new boots, I stamp the heel regretfully that I have not the feet of a statue I have seen — a Carpeaux nymph; it's another longing of mine! "

"So you would not care to be handsome for others' sakes?"

"First I would, and then I would not! Not for every one; for those whom I love only. One ought to be ugly for those one does not care for, whom one does not love, don't you think so, brother?"

Rendall had resumed his pencil work.

"What a fancy of yours, to long to be so un-English!" said he, after a moment's silence. "So dark!"

"And you—what do you long for, Signor Fiasco?"

"If I were a woman, I would long to be a little woman with neither brown nor light hair."

"Auburn then?"

"A dash of warm, and plump! as plump as a partridge!"

"'Whose plump little partridge would you be?' I am glad you said plump. I can breathe again. I was for one moment afraid of a declaration! It needed the sun to shine on your hair to remind me that you are forty."

"Forty! I was grey at five-and-twenty! if that is what you go by! I am only the third decade. But women always make men older than they are. But I can tell you yours precisely."

"I defy you to be mathematically correct!"

"Twelve! and you'll never be more!"

"Thank you, my friend, that's my heart's desire!" said Marcia fervently, "for I can then utter all the nonsense that flutters in my kaleidoscopic head. Carroll!" she continued, after some silence, "have you ever been in love?" Drawing back a little from her canvas she looked at it with her head on one side, like a bird suspicious of its seed, to see the effect of the last brushfull laid on.

"Miss Twelve-year old is beginning well!" replied the young professor. "What a question!"

"Well! and what of it? I ask you this, just as I'd ask you if you ever ate iguanas? It seems to me there's nothing forbidding in the subject. Can't you ask such questions in the present day? Come, Carroll; you say I am twelve, but unfortunately I am twenty I am a young lady; but if you imagine that young ladies of my age have never read novels nor sung love songs—that's humbug, balderdash! Well, as you like, but if you don't think me old enough, I revoke my question. I was thinking we were a couple of students talking in the *atelier!*"

"Well, since you are determined to extract an answer: I have been in love."

"Did you feel good?"

"Gracious! you girl, you have only to read again those novels, you will find my impressions in every page"

"But that is precisely what puzzles me most; every book you read is full of love, nothing else! And yet in actual life you don't see it. I, at all events, see none of it. On the contrary I see every one doing very well indeed without it. When we were at Scarborough, I could not help pointing out to papa such a well chosen couple, young, hand-

some, smiling, engrossed in one another, an ideal of
Paul and Virginia under a Turkey-red parasol ;
and, though papa hushed me, the chambermaid
told me !   What do you think they were ? "

" Pickpockets ? "

" You are a wizard.   They were professional
swindlers ; have been married eight years, and
spent half the time in prison ! What a disillusion !
I concluded that love exists in books alone—only
in the author's imagination."

Her companion laughed. " Marcia, since we
are here as fellow painters, as you say, and we
are talking frankly, like old friends, will you
allow me to ask you in my turn, if you have ever
felt, I will not say, love, but—but any strong
inclination for any one ? "

" Up to date ? No, never," replied she, after
a moment's reflection. " But I am no fair subject
—even for your pencil ! I believe such things
happen chiefly to people whose hearts are empty
orphans, lonely spirits, who are not filled with
such an affection as one cherishes for father or
mother."

Rendall made no remark.

" Don't you think that such affection is a pre-
servative?" said Marcia. " It's a cardiac vaccination!
Well, I assure you I try in vain to recollect any
one disputing my love for my father In school
when other girls treasured little relics of boys in
round collars, I never had anything in a locket

but papa's portrait, in such a high collar, ha, ha!
and, yes, a page of an illustrated paper, which
some one told me was the picture of a battle
wherein he pranced about. There was one officer
on a grey horse that I thought something like my
miniature, and I kissed it till the ink was worn
off."

"And later, when you had grown up?"

"Later—I have always been a child on this
subject. No, nothing, not an impression can I
recollect. That is to say, I am going to be perfectly candid with you—I had a little, a very
little beginning of what you say, a little of that
feeling which I afterwards found in stories, can
you guess in three goes only—for whom?"

"No, not in thirty."

"Why, for you, stupid! Oh, it was only for a
passing instant. I soon loved you in a very
different way, and a better one. I did not like
you at first. You seemed so severe, so reserved,
but I soon felt esteem and gratitude. I loved
you for having patiently and so politely corrected
my faults—spoilt child that I am! for having
opened my mind—for having inspired me with
fine, noble, generous sentiments, all through the
medium of sarcasm—jests that bite; but so does
mustard bite, and does it not help cold beef to
go down?" here she smacked her lips like a
cannibal. "I used to paint such namby-pamby
things, and though I stick to flowers and fruit,

and such fiddlededees, it is merely to keep my
hand going till I see my way clear to six months
on a historical scene. You set me to marking
down such noble subjects in poets which I turned
over as dry before you pointed out their beauties.
You have given me your contempt for croquet and
lawn-tennis, and I do prefer hand-ball against
the side of the works when the men are all in and
can't see me—that's the old English racquet, is it
not? And I took to rowing, and sailing, and
swimming, and try to jest like you, to tilt at
everything base, wicked, foolish, worthless, vile,
and mean. I try men by the fire-test, so to say,
and am so disgusted with simpletons! Much of
what I think, much of what I am, some little of
my petty value, I owe to you, Carroll Rendall.
I have wished to make you some return by a good
and steadfast friendship, bestowing on you cor-
dially as on a comrade—in my father's sense of
camaraderie—something of the love I have for
him, God bless him!" In speaking these last
words her voice assumed a lower note and a
graver tone.

"What's this?" interrupted the colonel, as he
strayed in, and cast his eye on Rendall's sketch.
"My daughter! 'Tis a frightful caricature!"
Seizing the sketch-book, he began tearing the leaf
out.

"Oh, you rough papa!" cried Marcia; "I wanted
to have it for a memento of how ugly I am."

CHAPTER XII.

A WAGONETTE was taking the Pleasantons on the road to Beechbrake, where Mr. Millward had a North Italian villa in Caen stone. Marcia had taken the whip and reins from the hands of her father, who was smoking a black briarwood by her side.

Enlivened by the drive, the air, and motion, Colonel Pleasanton shot his jokes on incidents of the drive, and gaily saluted all they met. His wife was in a brown study, preparing and rehearsing for her reception at the golden lion's den.

"But, mamma," said the charioteer, "you are saying nothing. Don't you enjoy the journey?"

"Yes, very much, very much indeed," replied Mrs. Pleasanton; "but I must tell you that this visit troubles me a deal; and if it were not for Henry, I should not undertake it. Miss Millward is so frigid. There is such imposing show in their mansion, to those ignorant how the owner amassed his wealth. He purchased some invention from a poor workman for next to nothing, and it has been a gold mine."

"Come now, Lotte," murmured the colonel. "Millward must have purchased more than one invention, unless it was an invention of the enemy—"

"Well, in spite of all that, I never feel at ease among these people."

"You are very good indeed, to sorrow so much about them!"

"That for their grand airs!" said Miss Pleasanton, touching up the horse with the whip, whereupon he instantly started off at a good rate.

There was just cause for Mrs. Pleasanton's terror. In the mansion, to which she was going, everything was calculated to intimidate, depreciate, and overwhelm guests with the feeling of their inferiority. There was a studied display, a skilful theatrical arrangement of opulence which aimed at the humiliation of others by violent contrasts, by the eccentricity of costly furniture, and rare antique ornaments. The height of the ceilings, the width of the stairs, the breadth of the window-panes, the superbly impertinent air of the footmen, their chief and two lieutenants in the ante-chamber, the massive plate on the sideboards, all intended to damp the man who had been arrogant on his paltry four or five thousand a year. Even when there was no company, father and daughters sat down to table in full dress, as if he was a German princeling — serene something ending in *esse*, lording it at his little court.

The proprietor and his elder daughter were in harmony with, and maintained the tone of their house. The spirit of their private life, their style of living became, as it were, second nature. The father with all he had "borrowed" from the nobility in return for the cash he had lent them; his manners, his attire, his curled beard like the prince, his superficial polish; his daughter with her grand airs, her supreme fastidiousness, all the tiresome absurdities of the rich middle-class, admirably represented inordinate plutocratic self-valuation. Such scornful politeness and haughty condescension seemed to lower themselves in the least act towards others. There was a sort of insolence in their very tastes. Millward Hall had no pictures nor objects of art. Mr. Millward's collection was of precious stones, amongst which he exhibited a ruby above price, since it was not in the market, mentioned in all works upon historical gems, one of the finest in Europe. Where paintings should have been on the walls, were decorative fantasies, Japanese incised panels, peacocks' feathers in inlay, Murano tablets, and such artistic splendours, degraded when displayed by the square yard.

Fashion had stamped all this display of wealth, and Millward Hall, brought into notice by its very marked peculiarities, was one of the three or four great modern show places for American tourists just out of London. It became the plutocrat's fixed abode after two or three winters passed at Nice under the pretext of ill-health, in the villa "Taud:iaco," a kind of *caravanserai*, open to all the great, rich, and celebrated who travelled that way. On great concert days, Cicely Millward displayed her fine voice and musical talents, all very so-so ; but the refreshing coolness of her sandwiching herself between Madame Patti and Madame Nillson was only paralleled by the stare of surprise she gave the Yankee impresario who, just to oblige his banker, a friend of Millward's, asked her what were her terms for a tour through the States, Sandwich Islands, and Havana! On these occasions European stars encountered Parisian reputations ; the world of science and transcendental æsthetics elbowed the world of politics, which was repre- sented by a very compact band of Conservatives and Independents out of office, in whose ranks Henry Pleasanton had figured very assiduously for more than a year. To these might be added a few hard-headed young fellows, capable of out- jockeying a Yorkshire trainer, who expect to be statesmen in the next reign, and who were intro- duced by Millward to his heiress, the Trill-ionare, as they at once styled her ; for Millward was in- clined to worship the star of the future.

The son of a Deal fisherman and brandy smuggler, his origin and his name, which sug- gested a cottonopolite strain, had exasperated him in his youth against the nobility, and manufac- turers and government officials in general. He had met and fraternized with Pleasanton in Italy, after which he had associated with Herzen, and knew the true cause of Garibaldi's sudden " flit ' from London ; again, in the States, where he had profited immensely in army contracts, land purchases, and whisky distilling, and shipped him munitions of war when he was battling in South America. It is to be hoped that he sent sounder stuff than that consignment of preserved meats to Abyssinia, about which there was a question in the House, and one of those breezes in Fleet Street which are always mysteriously allayed.

At the period of the Reform agitation, the one when the Hyde Park railings went down like a single front of infantry before the Nordenfeld, the incipient millionaire took a fright. He was living in Connaught Terrace, and saw it all, and even heard a rogue in fustian cry out, " Weapons ? every one of these pickets will do for pikes !" Immediately, with ludicrous rapidity, his ideas underwent a change, and his political conscience spun round to the opposite point. He rushed to the doctrines of the whiff of grapeshot, he sought the protection of the Church as he would an additional police to guarantee his property from Radical covetousness.

Unfortunately, against this sudden and sincere conversion of Millward, his education or lack of it, his whole past life, writhed, struggled, and rebelled, breaking out by fits and starts. He would catch himself humming "A smuggling he would go!" "La Russie, qui est knoutée," and Garibaldi's hymn; and a nautical expletive had been known to expedite the martial stalk of a footman on a dire emergency.

"Give the reins to your father, Marcia," said Mrs. Pleasanton; "I should not like you to be seen driving. It looks so fast. I wish we had had the carriage and coachman."

They had arrived opposite a large and magnificent bronze gate, in front of which were electric lamps. The lodge was modelled after a Roman mortuary house in marble. The carriage having turned into an avenue strewn with tinted sand and passed by some splendid clumps of rhododendrons, drew up at the portico. Two servants opened the glass doors of the marble-floored passage, the lofty windows of which were shaded with foliage of exotics. Thence the visitors were ushered into a reception room hung with crimson watered silk, with nothing on its walls but a statue, in a mosaic niche, of the late Mrs. Millward in the character of "Welcome," by Professor Tabagghi. Through the open windows might be seen in a piece of water a brace of herons, the one live thing Mr. Millward tolerated—peacocks excepted—in his grounds, and that only on account of their chivalric relations.

When the new-comers entered the reception oom, Miss Millward, seated on a sofa, was listening to the Italian governess, who was reading aloud to her sister Naomi. Their father, leaning against the Nevada white and lemon gold-spangled quartz mantel-piece, was playing with his celebrated watch-chain, a string of graduated aqual marines. Naomi had the autograph copy of Manzoni's "The foreigner must go !" illuminated like a missal, and gorgeously bound, in her hand. Cicely, with large, somewhat cold blue eyes, arched eyebrows, bold prominent nose, a haughty projection of the lower part of her face, recalled the Faustinas of modern painters of Roman scenes. Naomi had brown, strongly defined eyebrows. Her large curved lashes revealed less ardent than dreamy blue eyes. As for the governess, to have done with her speedily, she was one of those old duennas whom life's storms have tossed about and worn away the angularities, so that they have no more distinguishing features than an old coin.

"Now this is kind of you," said Miss Millward, rising and advancing as far as the border of one of the diamonds of the marquetry in the middle of the room ; "our dear neighbours give us a welcome, graceful surprise. It seems to me an endless time since we had the pleasure of seeing you all." Henry had so timed it as to add himself to the party. "Dear Mrs. Pleasanton, you would have been strangers only for your son having the goodness not to neglect us, and to come to our

Monday evenings"—she shook Henry's hand longer than the others and less formally, as he bowed—"else we should not have known what had become of you."

"You are very good," began Mrs. Pleasanton, seating herself at a distance from the young hostess.

"Oh, pray come nearer," said the other, making room by her side.

"We have been putting off our visit from day to day, so that we might come all together. It is the bane of dwelling near one another; the ability to come anytime prevents one coming at all."

"Well now, that's too bad," replied Miss Millward; while Naomi and Marcia entered into chat. "Had we better move a hundred miles apart? And it is a downright shame to leave those two children,"—she pointed to the young girls—"who have grown up together, without seeing each other often."

"Dear Miss Millward," said Mrs. Pleasanton, as she looked at them, "how long it is since we used to see you three sharing a rage for charades?"

"By Jove!" thought the colonel, "she's charging without sending out a scout. It is much more my diplomacy than Mrs. Pleasanton's."

"Ha, ha, ha!" laughed the lady, "you cannot have forgotten"—an ingenious mode of telling Miss Millward that she was not so old after all—"how you used to take all the antimacassars and shawls in the house to dress up as Turks."

"Oh yes, indeed!" cried Marcia, smiling and turning towards Naomi, "our best was Jack-boot. I was discovered fishing, and hauled up the fish-jack, don't you see?—and for the second syllable, Cicely, being tall, was the Giant in the Seven league Boots! She put on papa's! Do you not remember?"

"I should think I do!" replied Naomi, smiling; "but it was you invented most of our words."

"I am delighted, Miss Millward, to find you so kindly disposed towards the very thing I have come to ask of you; for you must know now at once that my visit is not entirely purely cere-monious. I came to bring those girls together again! Marcia has such a desire for private theatricals; and on that she naturally thought of her playmate first of all. And if Mr. Mill-ward, would kindly allow his daughters to take part with mine, it would make the perform-ance quite a *fête de famille*," with a dropping of her voice before the Italian governess, for it is a trial to ventilate your French with foreigners in hearing.

At the first words of this overture Naomi, who while chatting with Marcia had let her hand rest in hers, suddenly withdrew it.

"I am sure papa thanks you for this friendly idea, dear madam," replied Miss Millward, "and I thank Marsie also. You could never have suggested any one thing to please me better. The practice will do Naomi a deal of good, I do believe, for the child is nervous to a degree that is really painful to others. Acting would accustom her a little to speak up, to come out of her shell. It will also be an excellent stimulus to her mind."

"But, Cicely, you know very well I have a bad memory, and then, the very idea of acting before a lot of people! No, I had rather not. I tell you, though, I do not mind, in a pretty George III. dress, selling programmes; there!"

The elder sister eyed her coldly. "The idea of imitating a front of-the-house harpy!"

"But, dear, if I were capable I would do anything," pleaded Naomi, "but I am sure I should only spoil a performance."

"I shall keep by you, and then you will do beautifully!"

Naomi bowed her head as usual when her sister set her fiat on a project.

Meanwhile, Mrs. Pleasanton was embarrassed, and had let her eyes wander on a Fortnightly which lay open by her side, on the edge of a little novelty in tables, furnished with noiseless electric mechanism, which forced the article to follow you or precede you if you touched the releasing spring, like a dog.

"Oh!" said Miss Millward, turning to her, "you explore a familiar country: that is your son's last article. I can read such heavy essays when

I know the author. And when do you expect to bring out the play ? "

"But must we think of it now ? I should be very sorry to pain Naomi."

"Oh ! say no more about that. Naomi has always great difficulty in making up her mind unassisted."

"But, see here," broke in Mr. Millward, who had been conversing with the colonel at the other end of the room ; "if Naomi has too strong an objection—"

"Objection ! pooh ! she is in her heart very grateful to you," said the tyrannical daughter to her guest, without answering her father directly. "We are always obliged to put on pressure to see her in company. But you have not told me when the performance is to take place ? "

"When do you think best, Marcia ? " asked Mrs. Pleasanton.

" Well, I think—let's see ; a month for rehearsals, twice a week, eh ? We would rehearse on whatever days are most convenient to you."

"We can manage that, if you come over," said Miss Millward. " How do you like "—with a pause, to show how much their time was taken up—"Mondays and Fridays, at two o'clock ? Will that fall in with Naomi's engagements, Mademoiselle Gogois ? " The question was put without a glance at the governess. " You might even go over with us, when the time comes for us to go to Gratchley. You see how easily the matter is settled! Now you'll stay and dine? Just as you are. We have had no fixtures for to-day, and no telegrams from town."

"Oh! we are so sorry, but that's impossible. We are bound to have company ourselves to-day."

"How unfortunate! But I believe you have not seen the new Ceylonese house—all Ceylon plants, some unknown to naturalists before Herr Grubertrauel brought them over. I must gather you a bouquet, Marsie, pet! There is one flower —supposed to chew up little birds like a wild animal—a monstrous beauty, with two black spots on a yellow ground, like horrid eyes ; most fascinating. This is the way!"

"Let us clear, too," said Mr. Millward, pointing to a corridor entrance which led to the billiard room. "We'll leave you, Henry, with the ladies, to protect them from the vampire-flower. We can smoke here," continued the host, when the two elderly gentlemen stood cue in hand in their waistcoats, which, stripping for combat, enabled Millward to exhibit braces embroidered with seed pearls, like an Albanian princeling. "Those cigars are what you sent me from Caraccas, improved by seasoning ; though I never thought them capable of amelioration. The trouble I have had to keep my titled friends from robbing me of the lot! American game?"

"Yes, but I am out of fettle."

"You don't keep the ball a-rolling ; ha, ha ! eh ? "

" No ; no table."

"Unusual, is it not now ?   Billiards is not taboo'd ? " he inquired earnestly.

" No, only in my place. My son does not fancy any spot where balls are knocking about, " with bitterness.

" The boys don't now—afraid of getting a front tooth damaged."

" And as my wife does not think it a suitable amusement for Marcia—"

" She might do worse.   You have let me in for a good thing—I don't mean on this table, for you've spoilt the lay of the red for my favourite stroke —but with that busking work !   Where's the stage to be, here or in your house ?   Not here, I hope—I am disgusted with workmen ; no con- sciences.   It is impossible to get anything civilly done now.   You are at Johnny Ludlow's mercy. The other day, I had a decorator down from Shacknasty and Palmavecchio's, to set up some glasswork—rather fineish cobbling—on the west staircase, and, happening to be coming down while I was there, I saw he hadn't a lozenge of ruby quite flush in the leading, and, naturally, said : ' My fine fellow, that is not level true ! '   Twenty years ago, he would have replied : ' Werry good, sir,' with a touch of the forehead, and ' 'to job hover the furnace, gov'nor.' But this artistic gentleman, speaking as correctly as a Society of Arts lecturer, straightened up, caught me fair and square in the eye with his, and said : ' This is Mr. Millward, I suppose ? You will excuse me, sir ; but I am engaged by Messrs. Shacknasty and Palmavecchio, who have every confidence in my abilities, and any complaints should be made to them direct.' It could not have happened differently in the Northern States, I wager. Your son being one of those political economists, asserts that strikes do the workmen no good. I tell you straight, colonel, and I have seen a good many, each time the workman gets some advantage, and the capitalist never gets that back. And don't you believe it they are squandering money in drink ! they dress better, go round to amusements more, rig their girls up amazingly, and are putting by money. There's that Merionethshire property I bought, with an exhausted tin mine. Bless me, if I have not had a regular offer with guarantees, from a band of miners to work the diggings for twenty years, on a royalty. They must have bought their champagne and pianos very low to have such a surplus. Happily, I am too old to see fifty years hence ; but they that see it will not be able to get a shoe-black at all. It will be Yankee land, all machinery I often tell my daughters, that they will soon have to brush their own hair. Five . seven . you can pot the red now. I told the inspector who was guarding the rioters, mostly boys, inside the Marble Arch, that it would be the best thing for property owners to hang them on the trees. When they grow up they will be a terror—that day when there is a barricade across Oxford Circus, and an Armstrong hundred-pounder topping the Duke of York's column from a popular barricade." He began to hum, waving his cue in time :

> " We are only lads that work at the forge,
> But we swing sledges, and yet—by George !
> The Old Sledge game we mean to play,
> And the Peacock Ward will run away ! "

The Peacock Ward is rather a good nickname for the West End, in Albany, New York. The song is Yankee, but the sentiment is hard at work in England all the same.

" You had not such notions some thirty years ago, when we first became acquainted, Godfrey ! " said the colonel with a smile.

" True—I had finer sentiments—too fine for practical use," was the answer as Millward rested an elbow on his cue. " Ah ! we were young then. Well I recollect how I used to hate the police ; me and Primly went out one night, quite like our dads, when the Charleys were about, to maul the p.c.'s. Ho, ho ! such a row we had in the Strand, where the Music Hall was built years after—where the Gaiety Theatre now stands. Cabmen, street sweepers, sweeps from White Horse Alley, mud-larks, all joined in, and three times they sent up to Bow Street for reinforcements. It was a miracle we escaped being locked up, but a milk-man put us in his trap, heels and heads sticking out between the churns, and drove us through ' the blues.' I think you knew Primly ? "

" He ran away with some of my money ! "

" Yes, he absconded with thirty thousand al-together. I met him—no mistake, though he was perfectly undenationalized, as your long-winded son would say—in Arcachon. He was passing as a Portuguese, the Conde da Braga, where he had a paper mill, coining money. Did I mark for you ? eleven was it ?—I am not his class—I cling to my country !—you will win. I thought I should like to have put one of the police truncheons and a door knocker in the corner stone of this house ! Game ! "

They donned their coats, and sipped a fancy American drink—ice, sugar, lemon-scented herbs, spice, and nine-tenths froth.

" How is the church getting on ? " inquired Pleasanton, restoring his cue to its place in the rack with the care of an old soldier forming a stack of muskets.

" We are up to the second joists. I thought I knew something of building, but it runs already over my estimate. After all, it's a prodigal gift to a place like Beechbrake ; and it will not fill my terrace on Scrubiton Slope with tenants—"

" As a polo ground would do ? " at which the old boys roared, as, in their mood, they would have revelled over an even less obvious pleasantry.

"I never found Miss Millward so agreeable," commented the colonel's wife, when they were in the wagonette again.

" What an odd fish Millward is," said Pleasanton. " Though as a billiard player he's not worth the trouble of playing. I might have given him thirty and beat him easy. He learnt very little in America."

" It was Naomi that I thought odd," said Marcia. " Did you notice, Henry, she did not wish to play the part ? But Cicely was like Bully Bottom, eager to play anything, where you would be on the stage."

Henry made no reply.

CHAPTER XIII.

THE AMATEURS REHEARSE.

ON the following Friday, Naomi came over to Gratchley alone, save for the automatic governess ; and she entered the drawing-room with a restless, almost bashful look of embarrassment. On the threshold she had given one glance round the room, and then, as if reassured by no gentlemen being present, had presented her forehead for Mrs. Pleasanton's salutation, and a cold cheek to Marcia's kisses. The latter, joyfully laughing, with playful and caressing gestures, had removed her friend's dust-proof, and taken off her hat.

"One moment," said she, swinging the charming little white toque trimmed with mauve flowers, on the tip of her finger, as Rendall entered. "This is Mr. Rendall, whom you saw some time ago—long enough not to delude us into belief we are kids, if that be not slang—query, Mademoiselle Gogois ?—and whom I introduce to you as our manager. Mr. Rendall is also our professor of elocution, prompter, and operator on the electric light, for our stage is to have the most recent improvements ! The *Swans* will make our geese—that's not courteous—make our geese hiss as gently as a sucking-dove! Mr. Rendall is a teetotum! no, he is not fond of a spin, I meant a factotum!"

"I have not forgotten you, sir," murmured Naomi. "You were kind to me when I was a little girl."

Colouring at this innocent remark more than Marcia at one of her villainous *jeux de mots*, Naomi offered the chemical authority a trembling hand, with a delightfully timid air.

"What a delicious frock!" cried Marcia, gently stroking the exquisitely-fitting dress, and pulling out her skirt from under the sash. "You will make an ideal little countess. I am going to be *that* jealous!" pointing to a Barbedienne Salvini as Othello. "That's a most becoming way to dress your hair. It makes you look taller. Your head seems on the level with mine," placing herself after the Wakefieldian precedent, back to back with her guest. "Look, mamma, she even tops me, eh?"

The governess had retired into a corner, as if a game of "puss" was proposed, and was looking at the pictures in an illustrated book.

"Come, my dear girls, suppose we begin to attend to your play?" said Mrs. Pleasanton. "We need not wait for Henry. He may have missed the train. And besides, he need not come until the last few rehearsals, when the others have learnt their parts. He is so quick at study."

"No, mamma, I would rather chatter right ahead, as Henry says Miss Vredenhosen, the latest American belle, terms it. Pray let us talk. Come here, Naomi; we have a lot of little confidences, ever so many characters to pull to pieces, since we were really by ourselves."

Whereupon Marcia began with her friend one of those warbling chit-chats, in which young girls love to indulge, now interrupted by a burst of laughter, or dying away in a whisper. Naomi, at first on the defensive, soon abandoned herself to the charm of this open-heartedness, and the two revelled in early recollections.

Mrs. Pleasanton analysed the pleats of the visitor's dress, counted the leaves and petals on the spray in her hat, estimated the length of the sash unfolded, and was contented in so spending the time. Mr. Rendall sauntered over to the Italian governess in her nook, and scrambled along in a parley, with his Tuscan, pronounced after his training in Latin.

"I still am fond of painting," said Marcia; "and your voice is all it bid fair to be."

"Oh, don't shake its terrible mane at me!" cried Naomi. "They make me sing often enough now. Cicely prevails on me to sing at her grand parties; and you have no idea how I shrink from it. I am put on the vocal *menu* like an *entrée* of plain English dumpling among superfine dainties. We have such ladies—queens of song, goddesses, come to sing sometimes. I sit and listen to them spellbound ; and when the applause awakens me I seem to have been in heaven—all spirit, and not a creature in jewels, gloves and bodice—listening to a celestial choir. They are very condescending to me, and praise me warmly ; but what a contempt they must feel, with their voices that fill a hall, for one who would be drowned if help was thirty feet away and life depended on her cry being heard! Now, Cicely can sing, and has a voice! and not the faintest fear! I have seen her stand up without a quaver though the piano stool broke, and let the accompanyist roll into papa's lap! I shall have an attack of stage-fright—I shall burst out crying and run off. I know I shall."

" But won't you lunch ? You can fancy some other delicacy than sour apples and Abernethies?"

" No, thanks, thanks, darling ; I am not hungry, indeed, after the drive."

" Hark! like the Italian organmen when you have no threepennies! What are you jabbering, Mr. Rendall ? You may flatter yourself that is the language of crystallized sunshine and perfume, but I don't."

Rendall laughed.

" You will not be in the way now—we have finished our little budget. You may come and talk to us—anything but mineralogy."

" Have you looked at your watch, Marcia, lately ? If you mean to begin rehearsal to-day—"

" ' Now's the day and now's the hour, see the front of Ma's to lower.'   Oh, mamma, don't spur a willing horse—it is warm to-day ; and, besides, it is Friday ! "

"And there are thirteen characters in the piece," said Rendall, in a sepulchral voice.

"What of that ? " asked Naomi, turning to him with a perplexed look at his doleful voice.

" Don't mind him, he is the funniest creature in the world, for all his gravity at other times.   I believe he does not study one bit, but has an imp in a whiskey bottle, and so is crammed with knowledge upon every subject."

" An Irish imp—the leprechaun, then ! "

" There he is again at his jokes.   He taught me to dislocate English in punning.   Well, we will rehearse at the next visit won't we ? we have oceans of time ! "

" Oceans ! " cried Rendall.   " I don't see it. Real actors would—"

" We are not real actors, and don't mean to be ! So that's done with.   Now enliven the conversation immediately, sir; and if you are very, very amusing, I'll give you an etching, one of my own—black, all black, but for one glaring dab of white, and innumerable little specks, and a cross line— 'Midnight on the Gratchley Water-Cutting,' the line being the towing-rope, and the white dab the barge ! "

" And the specks, sparks from the bargee's pipe ? '

" No, sir; stars.   A British Meryon ! "

"I prefer our Maid Marion. Pose as one in a forester's dress, and I'll draw you!"

"Yes; your last attempt at portrait-painting came to a nice end. Papa ground it to atoms!"

"Miss Millward," lamented the gentleman; "I choose you as umpire : this young Kauffman— Demonia, I can't say Angelica—has already given me a profile rosy apple, and a parsnip at full length —and by way of pendants, a robin's nest, not even edible—and a wedge of Swiss cheese. No doubt the intention was good, but my landlady declares my sitting-room looks like a greengrocer's shop."

"There's a sample of man's ingratitude to Art," said Marcia gaily to Naomi. "They are all ungrateful, dear. To think that you will be chained to some such unimpressionable monster before long ; for we are getting on."

"Not at rehearsal," cried Rendall.

"You be silent. We have heard enough of you. Have you any nice new duets? bring some over with you next time; or I'll go to you, and we will play them."

All of a sudden, the governess rose in her corner and interjected a "Four!" like a compound speaking and calculating machine. It was four clock, and there being a state dinner at Millward Hall, her charge was obliged to depart.

"First rehearsal over," observed Rendall. "It is just as well : I had not received the play-books by post."

CHAPTER XIV.

"ON this occasion, we mean business—stage business," enunciated Mr. Rendall. "Will Miss Naomi Millward stand there before the sideboard—so, or sit, if you prefer it. That's it. Now all ready to commence: 'The little Countess, Lord Edgardus Faulconhero, and Miss Pauline Pry discovered as the curtain rises.' Miss Pry— go on, Miss Pleasanton!"

"One moment, please; the fact is—"

"The first scene," hesitated Naomi; "I—I have not grasped the situation, as they say. I know the other better."

"So do I," observed Miss Millward.

"The second, then; page ten. Let us try the second. I shall take Henry's part—for this evening only," he added with some stress, which, however, no one but the eldest lady noticed, if she did so. "'Oh, my dear boy, if my love—'"

He was interrupted by a burst of laughter from Marcia.

"Good heavens," cried she to Naomi, "how comically you are placed! There's two plaques on the sideboard, one each side of you ; and, all in white, you look like a lump of sugar in the tongs."

"I ! A sweet simile," grumbled Naomi, with a twinge as if she felt the nippers in question, and changing her position hastily. "I wish she would not make her jokes before that Mr. Rendall, with his great all-observing eyes."

"Be kind enough not to interfere with the actors, Miss Pleasanton," said Rendall, perhaps sympathizing with Naomi. "'Oh, my dear boy, if my—'"

"Purse!" cried the irrepressible Marcia.

"Purse?—no, no—'love—'"

"The purse!" cried Marcia again. "You will require it."

"No, next page. But I thought you were to have it ready. There's my note : 'See, she enters with purse for Bus.'"

"I ? not at all ! On the contrary, it's you as property gentleman. You're a pretty stage manager, I should say! Cicely, what do you think of the donkey who wrote this piece ? A wife gives her husband her own money—hands him over the purse !"

"Do let us get on," moaned Rendall.

"Mr. Rendall, you utter that in the tone of a man who would like to leave the ladies, and join the hardened old smokers !"

"I always have a wish to smoke, Miss Pleasanton," replied the martyr; " especially when a cigar is prohibited. My German education makes me pipe mad."

" That's a failing of men ! forbidden fruit ! I have tasted papa's pipe—horrid.   What pleasure can you find in smoking ? "

" The pleasure found in petty vices; that illustrates mankind well. But, I beg your pardon, Miss Millward. To begin again. That's better. Now for Edgardo's entrance," and Marcia being quieted, the rehearsal proceeded.

The next one fell through, for the Millwards could not attend.

" And I looked forward to it so ! " wailed Marcia. " And Cicely getting so thawed out, at least to Mr. Rendall. I miss Naomi now that she has begun to love me again. I miss her as if she were one of us. I grant she is not amusing ; she sadly lacks vivacity, and she's not an intellectual marvel. How she does stare at an abrupt change in the conversation ! But I like her. She has such calmness, it soothes my nerves. And then her mere presence warms my heart. She is a thermal spring—her sister is a volcano ! "

" You are partly right, anyhow," agreed Mr. Rendall.   "The younger Miss Millward's dis-position is tender, very loving.   In such natures there is, as it were, a sympathetic current flowing towards others."

" When she was quite a little thing, I remember,

she was just the same, full of sensibility ; and how she used to weep—a warm spring, indeed !

" And how clearly her character is shown in her face ! You might almost say that her beauty is made up of tenderness and of what she still retains of her childhood. That's an air she particularly wears. I never could say an unkind word to her, snub her as her sister does ! And yet I am a cruel torment ! "

"This tenderness, nevertheless, is very extraordinary," said Mrs. Pleasanton.

" Why, no, it is easily explained," replied the chemical professor.   " She is too refined for her father to please her, and her sister is a selfish, overbearing Agrippina ! She once had a pinch of poverty, or, at least, misery; and she has determined to crush every emotion rather than run the risk of loss of fortune. Naomi has been penning up her love, and Marcia suddenly becomes the object."

" You're   another ! " cried   Marcia, laughing. " It is well such effusion is not over some man ! "

"I pity her," said Rendall.   " The man will appear up a trap ! The poor girl is so rich, so very rich."

" A great misfortune, truly ! " interrupted Mrs. Pleasanton.

"It is one of the greatest," replied the professor. " She might have been happy with love alone ; but her money will cause her nothing but a crushed heart."

The subject of this discourse remained ignorant of it, of course, and was happy in the society
f Marcia during the fortnight which was spent in
.hose eminently practical rehearsals. Still Henry
did not come on the scene; and at last, Miss
Millward remarked the continued absence.

"Oh, Henry is like lightning for learning anything," said the complacent mother; "he will be
perfect in a couple of rehearsals."

"Very likely; but it is hard on Mr. Rendall
to read the part every time," said Miss Millward.
"I confess, however, that I tremble for poor
Naomi, though you may be tolerably satisfied with
her. It will be so necessary to do it well, after you
have kindly let us put the theatre up on our
lawn. It holds four hundred seated! quite an
audience!" she concluded, with the vanity of
wealth.

"You really must come to rehearsals, Mr.
Pleasanton," said Rendall, that evening.

"If I must, I must," was the reply, ungra-
ciously. "I wish any other idea had been put
on the stage. I have been in two scuffles, actual
scuffles, already over it. They were talking about
it in the Chatham, and Sowerbee, who will have
no ticket, and knew he had no hopes, asked with
that droop of his left eyelid, which is as rude as a
lear: 'What's the *pièce de resistance*, Henry?
Sullivan's "*Contrabandistas?*"' Right before a
newspaper fellow who is writing 'Scum on the

South Coast,' and is hungry for material about
the old smuggler — I daresay you have heard
some false yarn of her father having dabbled in
French brandy and Brussels lace during those
forgotten wars with Bonaparte.   And again, in the
very doorway of the Etoile Restaurant, when I had
Dauntless on my arm, old Major Bouncable said
he understood our theatre was fitted up like Drury
Lane—' By Jove, Dauntless ! they are going to do
that old Coburg blood-and-thunder drama, " The
Idiot of the Mountain ! "' a nasty slap at the ladies."

"No, no !" cried Rendall, flushing, but recog-
nizing the impossibility of Marcia being accused
of imbecility.   " It is a male character, I rather
fancy, a boy or so."

"Maybe.   But he meant Naomi Millward.   She
has no reputation as a wise-acre.   If it had been
one of those foreign countries where duelling
is possible, I should have urged Millward to call
the Major out."

" So you approve of duelling on some grounds
—foreign grounds, perhaps?" queried Rendall,
carelessly, his thoughts already in town, where he
expected, on seeing the major, to give him a piece
of his mind.

" No, no ! it's a reprehensible practice.   Pray
heaven, I never take a life."

" Nevertheless, there are times when—"

But the argument ceased there.   The younger
Pleasanton was already skimming his " part."   In

a week he was ready. As Miss Millward objected to any other performers, even vocalists, between the acts, and "One Fool makes Many" played "too short" to give the *chef* time duly to elaborate the hot dishes, it was proposed to finish the performance with a ballet pantomime. But not one of the vulgar mixtures of "knockabout" clowns and awkward dancing girls only seen in music halls; this would never do for Millward Hall. On the contrary, Henry had unearthed dresses, music and all, described for the "Harlequin Treasure-finder" of Bensérade and Lulli, and the gentleman who assisted him in French essays, an ex-Communard, found an artist, who designed the costumes in quite ultra-Britannic taste as to the length of the petticoats. It was pronounced a novelty, and South Kensingtonia wept her eyes out with spite at not having thought of it, when she saw the costumes of the Twelve Hours, being the *corps de ballet,* and those of Arlequina and Colombine in the show-rooms of Madame Phinaiguille. They had a wiry little creature down from a London theatre for the Colombine, which no one dared to undertake, and, with the persevering patience of the Jewish race, from which she nimbly sprang, Miss Ninavite taught Miss Naomi Millward to play the not onerous character of Arlequinetta. We may say that the Treasure of which the hero was in search was nothing more nor less than a loving heart.

Captain Router was to have been the harlequin
(and, indeed, he had recommended Miss Ninavite),
having a reputation for cutting capers in garrison
towns where they have a regular theatre ; but
some tyrant at the Horse Guards, concluding that
a man who could pirouette and support even a
prima ballerina of seven stone on his knee in
the tableau, deserved revocation of his sick leave,
called him back to quarters, and Henry Pleasanton
volunteered to wield the lath and wear the sable
vizard, in spite of the sudden, fierce, and inex-
plicable opposition of Miss Millward. Naomi, on
the other hand, seemed pleased to have a neighbour substituted for the strange captain. Indeed,
since Henry joined the company, so to say,
Miss Naomi Millward's character seemed totally
changed. Marcia was astonished to see a spirit
of contradiction which she had not discovered
before. She was hurt, too, at the air which Naomi
assumed towards her brother, a coolness, with a
shade of disdain almost contemptuous. And Cicely
lost all that amiability which had almost eclipsed
her pride. She seemed to watch young Pleasanton
very closely when he and her sister were together
—and, it must be confessed, Mrs. Pleasanton con-
trived such *tête-à-têtes* very dextrously.

Still, Marcia's brother was very polite, obliging,
and attentive to both the girls, but nothing more,
to his sister's perception ; and all the while he
played with Naomi, he even threw in so much

reserve, so much restraint, that Marcia fearful for the success of the performance, and dreading the coldness of his acting in such a lively part as harlequin, joked him about it.

"My dear Marsie," replied he," I am like the real actors. I never show what I am going to do at rehearsals. I shall come out strong when the curtain is up."

CHAPTER XV.

MR. MILLWARD had not done things by halves. The theatre in the grounds resembled one of those fantasies in scenic architecture which the artists of the Renaissance attached to Grand Dukes of spectacular tastes, designed, if they did not carry them out. There was a sliding roof, in the event of our climate whisking the needle round from fair to wet. A row of shrubs with variegated leaves had been left before the front of the stage to temper down the rays of the electric footlights.

Marcia painted the curtain, with assistants. It was a tolerably faithful representation of a view she had sketched at Elmwood. At either side of the theatre two papier-mache Fames had flags suspended from their six feet trumpets, like a herald's, with the bill of the play emblazoned in gold :—

For this Night Only !

THE COMEDIETTA :

"ONE FOOL MAKES MANY."

To conclude with

"HARLEQUIN TREASURE-SEEKER,"

BALLET PANTOMIME

(First time in 100 years).

Vivat Regina.

On every chair in the house, in front of the stage, sat the fashionable concourse, the names to be seen in the *Post* and Society organs, if you have a curiosity that way.

The curtain rose on the Comedietta. Marcia acted the part of a kind of amateur Rosa Bonheur who doated on animals, with much animation ; Miss Boxby was inoffensive as Miss Parbuckle, and little La Ramoli exquisite as a saucy Abigail. As the siesta-loving husband, Henry Pleasanton proved himself one of those clever amateurs who are often to be found amongst reserved fellows and grave men of the world, actors already in their own way. Naomi herself, bolstered up by Henry's acting, deftly prompted from P.S. proscenium entrance, by Rendall, and somewhat galvanized by the large assemblage, succeeded tolerably well in an affecting part of a neglected wife. This was a great relief to Cicely, who had a character of the Marble Heart description, with occasional outpourings of the true fiery temperament beneath. She frightened her sister into playing well, after the manner in which Señor Garcia showed his daughter Malibran that he wore a pointed dagger in " Othello" for the purpose of killing Desdemona veritably, if she made a *fiasco*. Naomi never breathed at peace till the curtain fell the last time, to applause, if not ear-rending, glove-splitting enough for even a Millward's content.

Cicely Millward hastened to change her dress and come to her place next her father in the first row, quite overjoyed at the undeniable success. After receiving gratulations, she reposed while the secreted band played amid noisy confusion of voices, offering opinions and meek criticisms, which at amateur threatricals succeeds the first applause. In the midst of all, Cicely caught vaguely some sentence spoken near enough to startle her, and one, later, distinctly reached her ear : " Yes, 'tis his sister, I know ; but I think, for the character he is not sufficiently in love with her—and certainly showed too much love for his wife." The woman who spoke, perceiving that the hostess was on the alert, bent towards her neighbour's ear to complete her comment. Cicely became serious, and heedless of her father.

After a long wait, of course, the curtain rose again ; and Henry Pleasanton reappeared as harlequin, the old French Opera-Italien Arlequin, with loose pantaloons, and a two-cocked drab felt hat, not Rich's innovation to which we are accustomed. He glistened with diamond dust.

A general stir was observed amongst the ladies, announcing that the costume and the actor were considered charming, and no such excitement arose again till Miss Ninavite came on the boards, for whom there was the success of curiosity, enhanced when the very magnificent diamond necklace which Millward had presented her for training his daughters, flashed and corruscated in glaring discord with her character as columbine. But these things will happen at amateur theatricals, and, as Rendall remarked—for he was not required in the pantomime, and also came round to the front of the house (they had stage slang so fluent on the tongue!)—"Miss Naomi Millward may ride in a gilded carriage, and so I do not see why there is a murmur at her jewelled 'coach.'"

This by the way.

The *Arlequinade Musicale* was an absurd legend of the hero scampering about here and there, aided and abetted by Arlequina, in search of a treasure, the upshot being an old wizard's (who stuck in the trap cauldron, it is true, when he was shot up) apparition to point to Columbine and make it clear that her heart was the true riches every man should covet. As innocent as a fable of Florian. The dozen young ladies who represented the hours, and paced a rigadoon, wore all their trinkets, and the hooped satin petticoats hardly exhibited more than their ankles, and not more than one pair slightly thick among the twenty-four, which was amply satisfactory.

Columbine was as pretty as a marmoset, and nimble as a squirrel, but the assemblage gave her little attention, if we except the gentlemen along the wall ; and yet they had seen her before. Mrs. Pleasanton and some rascals whom Mr. Blandford, (who had come down with a whole railway carriage of his patrons) had begun the plot which underlaid the frivolities. They centred the interest upon Arlequina and her constant companion, and pretty soon there was a buzz that signified that these two were the true hero and heroine. When the scene came where Arlequin had to be taught how to make love by Arlequina, and then to repeat the mimicry to show that he had learned the lesson perfectly, there was sympathetic applause. Even the young fellows who had never dared dream of a conquest of the stately Miss Millward being possible, thought Henry deserved the younger sister for this public and " artistic " exhibition of his sentiments towards her.

Around Mrs. Pleasanton, Blandford, and Cicely, there was an air of enchantment, diffusing through the auditorium, a sympathetic complicity of the audience encouraging the young couple to love each other. The *Minuet de la Mariée* was danced charmingly by the pair and applauded, but from the moment Henry was paired off with the professional columbine, there was a slackening of interest. When the curtain fell with a flourish of violins worthy of Lulli's own band, a few noticed the Arlequin dart one fond glance at Arlequina, as if he regretted, in all his blissful future with his prize, that his first love was to be seen no more. The curtain roller fell hard and bounded with a thud. Miss Millward's deep sigh was thus unheard, but everybody near her saw her fall fainting into her father's arms.

" You can leave me," said she to those surrounding her where they had carried her into the fresh air of the garden. " It is over. It was nothing but the relief at all succeeding so completely, and the heat ! "

She was quite pale, but smiled.

" I need nothing but a little air. Let Mademoil selle Gogois walk with me to the end of the grounds, and I shall meet you in the house as well as ever."

The creaking of their footsteps on the grave, had scarcely ceased, when she dismissed the governess, and stealing up to what might be called the stage-door of the temporary theatre, waylaid the Arlequin. " Henry, you love my sister ! " she said, gripping his arm feverishly. " Don't deny that you love her ? "

" Why, Miss Millward, I—" began the man but not startled, though the clutch pained him.

"Be silent! you cannot lie!" She pushed away his arm. Pleasanton bowed. "I see all. Look at me!" She searched his eyes with hers, and he hung his head. "Say something in your own defence! Can you not speak? can you not continue your acting off the stage?"

"It is because I have no reason to defend myself, Cicely," said the young man with his clear and gentle voice. The great heiress drew back at the familiar name, as if he had still further shocked her. "I have struggled for a long time to resist the temptation," resumed Pleasanton. "I don't excuse myself for playing false to you, but I am a sort of shark that exists without a heart. At least, I thought so; but now I find I have a heart for Naomi. I must acquaint you with the truth. I love your sister, it is but too true, and I reap one consolation from it: no one can call me a money-hunter, now, as ere I kept away from you at the time our affection was bruited about."

"But you have never communed with her before these accursed theatricals! What a scheme of yours, your mother, and your sister! How I have been gulled! Why, you hardly looked at her when you did come down to the Hall. What is it attracts such men, if not money? tell me! Do you think her handsome, like me, even in her insipid style? You fools! Did my condescension turn your head? Can such as she, poor child, flatter your pride, feed your vanity, and serve your ambition ? for you are ambitious, Mr. Henry Pleasanton! the women who will sacrifice feminine vanities and home joys to advance a politician, are found only once in a life time. Read your notes of our age! And it is only by women of my stamp, grand women, that insignificances like yourself can be led into salons where the giants of Russia and the colossi of Germany, the dashing cavaliers of Hungary, and the American senators, seven feet tall, reduce such clerk-looking men into pigmies! I love you? I loved your prospects! But a truce to this; we will be missed in the house. I tell you that, materially, you mistake in loving her : she is not rich, not well off even, if I once become her enemy."

" For shame, Miss Millward !"

" Would I spare the fly that stung me, because it was so small? Be she my stinging gnat, and I'll demolish her! I'll deprive her of her patrimony."

"Be still, for God's sake! There's that governess! I entreat of you, for your own sake—hers—your father's! A window has just been opened on the lawn."

"Composure is a very fine thing, Mr. Pleasanton," said the infuriated lady. "But look overhead: after calm, tempest. Henry, there is going to be a storm."

Indeed, menacing clouds were careering over

the sky, one melting into another, and blotting out the stars. She gazed into the gathering darkness, like Ajax defying the bolt, and seeking the point whence the thunder would be hurled.

" Mr. Pleasanton, it will come, and nothing either you or that silly child may do can hold back the scathing fire ! "

She turned towards the mansion, whither he followed her.

" Naturally, sir, we never meet again," said she without looking back.

Passing a fountain, she handed him her handkerchief. "Wet that for me," she commanded.

He knelt on the edge, and gave her back the moistened lump of lace, as it had become. She dabbed her forehead and her eyes with it, and calmly added: "Now I can go in, give me your arm. I hope my voice is more steady, since I promised to sing ' Break ! break ! break ! ' "

A few minutes subsequently, Miss Millward was singing with her enviable contralto, wearing that heroic smile under which " fashionable " actresses conceal the tears they shed in secret, and the wounds which rankle in their hearts.

Henry Pleasanton excused himself from going home. On the contrary, he went up by the one a.m. special, into which he had had some baskets of champagne conveyed, and the noisy hilarity alarmed peaceful stations along the line.

"I don't know," said Major Bouncable, on reeling out and being saved from going under the footboard by Blandford's ready arm, "what has come over Pleasanton. All the way up he has been raising the devil."

"I believe you, Major, my boy!" said the agent, going home in a cab alone. "He *has* raised the devil!"

CHAPTER XVI.

LIKE MOTHER, LIKE SON.

" MARSIE!" said Mrs. Pleasanton to her daughter one evening, "will you come with me to-morrow to see the new picture gallery, the London Assembly of Arts? It's very curious, they all say. I understand one picture cost six thousand guineas: 'The Descent of the Imperial Gladiator into the Arena,' by some foreigner. Mr. Perch thinks it would interest you. He has sent me the illustrated catalogue, and a season ticket. Will you go?"

"I should like it very much," replied the girl, smiling.

Next day Marcia was rather surprised to see her mother enter the room when she was dressing, and to observe the care with which she commented upon her toilette.

"You see, darling, exhibitions are so fashionable lately," said she, "you must look your best."

The Gallery of the Assembly of all the Arts was the freshest outcome of the artistic dealer's ferment; there were pictures, of course, though they were not the attraction, statues, curios, knick-knacks, a sort of " free lunch," for the prices were ridiculously moderate for delicacies not often seen on a public exhibition buffeteer's tariff-table, and soft music stealing in from an American organ hidden in a forest of tropical foliage. Needless to say there were plenty of lounges, and lenses of incalculable power for the weak-sighted.

The colonel's wife and daughter found Mr. Perch awaiting them, who, giving his arm to the elder lady, took a turn with them round the room. He led them to the paintings signed by the most celebrated names in Europe, simply explained the subject of each, without talking Painting. Marcia was obliged to him the more without knowing why. Having made the circuit, they released Mr. Perch. They chatted a while with him, and then, leaving Mrs. Pleasanton on a lounge, the old man and the young girl went off to view some statuary.

All know the impossibility of sitting among portraits without the eyes of one in particular, sooner or later, seeming to fall upon you, causing a painful impression that you are being stead-fastly watched. This sensation affected Mrs. Pleasanton, who abruptly overcame the spell, and lifted her gaze towards a portrait opposite her.

" How like my Henry ! " was her first ejacula-tion.

Her eyes were fairly good, but she took up

one of the magnifiers, and instantly started back
as the face loomed up—the *image* was a *simula-
crum* of her boy! She rose with a pale face,
forgetting the catalogue would have informed her,
and staggered to the picture. At the bottom of
the frame, incised on a shield held between the
Basilisks, which are the world-renowned sup-
porters of the Fairfield family, she read : "Madame
the Countess of Fairfield." Then there rushed
upon her memory the tale Mr. Blandford had told
her, to explain his having the diamonds in the
jewel-case, and she shrank back shuddering. As
a wild animal afar from the lair, at hearing a
hunter's gun fire, has no thought but to flee back
to her little ones, she prepared to dart away. " She
seeks her child : she has limitless wealth! Oh,
am I to lose him now!" She hastened to where
Mr. Perch was pointing out the details of a
Meissonier, and, pale and trembling, cried :

"Marsie, let us go, you have seen them all!" and
Mrs. Pleasanton dragged her daughter away, without a rest till they were at the head of Old
Hurlingham Street, when she moderated her gait,
so that they should not enter her " dentist's " in
that unaccountably frenzied way which had perplexed poor Mr. Perch. Immediately after a brief
interview with the agent, principally spent in
reminiscences of the fête at Millward Hall, with
some phrases of hidden meaning for Marcia, they
went home. The early return might have been

an annoyance to Miss Pleasanton, but it was a joyous relief to Naomi, who had been in despair at arriving at Gratchley and finding Marcia gone.

The girls rushed into one another's arms, and keeping them about their waists, went into the garden so intertwined. Mrs. Pleasanton sought her own room, with a headache.

With a very tragic aspect indeed, for one recently the Harlequina, Miss Millward suddenly moaned: "I've a secret to tell you, dear."

Marcia looked at her with amused surprise.

"So have I one for you, unless it is the same," she observed, kissing her. "I overheard some words between my father and mother. They were talking of my brother. But sit down; I'm tired with the shaking of the train."

They sat down on a garden seat.

"But you are crying! What is the matter?" said Marcia.

The girl's head fell on her shoulder, and she burst into tears, which rained warm and fast on her friend's hand.

"What is there wrong? Oh, tell me! answer —speak to me, Naomi! Come, out with the thorns, my little pet!"

"Oh, you don't know," replied Naomi, in heart-broken words, and gasping for breath. "Can't you save me?" and she threw herself despairingly on the other's neck. "I love *you* more than ever, though I ought not!"

"Well, child, you soar out of my ¡reach! Is it true then, that a marriage is debated? Is it my brother who will be engaged to you? I wish you would answer me."

"I wish I were dead."

"Dead! Why? you wicked one!"

"Because your brother loves another."

She recoiled before the horror of a complete discovery of what she feared or suspected, and then seeing Marcia bewildered, finished her revelation by a whisper, till sinking her head on her friend's bosom, she hid the shame of her soul and the blush on her cheek.

"My brother loves Cicely, and courts you! You can't say so! it is false!" and pushing her away with one bound, Marcia stood erect before her, like Hamilton's Cassandra.

Naomi's only answer was a gentle but steady look at the speaker, with dilated eyes in which truth shone with a steady light.

Before that gaze Marcia folded her arms, stood paralyzed for a few moments, silent, but it was a resolute, collected attitude. She felt the strength of a woman, and almost the duties of a mother towards that wronged girl. It was she who spoke first, and thus:

"But what does your father say to it? My brother has no money, no position to justify a union even with you?"

"But he is to purchase an estate, change his

name, and after a little while be given the title
which no Government can or will give my father.
I know not the objection."

"Let me consider. There is some mystery
here. If your sister loves my brother—if Henry
loves her—if he is a money worshipper, why did
he not propose to her? She is the heiress! you
will have only the money your father chooses to
bestow on you."

"But I am the heiress! Don't ask me why,
for I cannot even guess! but I am the heiress
of my father's estate."

"Naomi, weep no more! I'll have this made
right when next I meet this admirable brother of
mine."

CHAPTER XVII

IT was that night.

"Yah!" yawned Henry Pleasanton on the verandah. "Is that you, Marcia?"

He was smoking in that blissful state of a man who, buried in an arm-chair, with his slippered feet on the rail above the ordinary position, sees seraphic faces in the ascending rings of vapour.

He was thinking over all that had occurred within the last few months. He congratulated himself on having manœuvred like a Talleyrand. He recalled to mind that idea of the afterpiece, and the captain's sudden removal in his favour. His absence from the early rehearsals, the frigid indifference towards Naomi to pique her, and yet to lull any aversion, to arrest on her lips a refusal to act with him. He thought on that masterstroke, his love suddenly revealed to the public, though to the sister's jealousy, in the midst of the splendour of the play, escaping from him as if the part which he was playing wrested away the secret of his very heart. No one ever compromised a girl more glaringly, yet so uncensurably. What followed, the way in which he had driven his dupe to the verge of despair, his restraint during the final interview— all this came back to his recollection, and he felt a sort of pride in himself, as he recalled so many circumstances foreseen, combined, arranged beforehand, and so naturally brought to bear and operate on the passion of the majestic girl.

"It is I, Henry! I have no inclination for sleep to-night," said Marcia gravely, almost solemnly, drawing a chair out to sit down on it. "I want to gossip, as we used to do once upon a time, if you remember, when you had no home in town. What pleasant chats we had here when everybody else was asleep! How often we laughed! what nonsense we prattled in this open porch, like blacks in a *corrobaree!* Am I right? My brother is a man, a man who has done with laughing."

"Yes, things are serious!" avowed Henry smilingly; "I am going to get married."

"Oh!" said she, "it is all true. But it is not too late! I implore you," she ran on, throwing herself on her knees to seize his hand, "Oh, you would not do that, for mere money! I am at your feet, look! And to give up the name of one's honourable, glorious father—a hero not appreciated in his own country yet; but Mr. Rendall read to me from a South American paper that they have put up a statue to him and their compatriot, his comrade, General Arnold, before th

Church of the Christian Graces, in Puerto Cabello ; and little children kneel to it, and bless the Englishman who spilt his blood, our blood, brother Henry, for a country not his own ! Oh, do not take a step further towards the altar with that young lady, that child ! I beseech you, if you love our father, if you love me, if you love us all ! oh, I beseech you."

" Are you going mad, girl ? What's all this scene about ? Pray, get up ; we have had enough of theatricals lately, I thought."

Marcia rose, and fixing her hot eyes, when the tears had dried up, on her brother's face, she said, " Naomi has told me everything ! "

The colour mounted to his cheeks, and then he became deadly pale, as if a man had slapped his face with a glove.

" You cannot marry Miss Millward, or Naomi, now ! " she cried.

" If Naomi told you so, she *is* an idiot ! My dear goose," continued Pleasanton in an agitated voice, " it seems to me that you are meddling with affairs that don't concern you ; and you will allow me to tell you that Miss Millward is pre-eminently calculated to fight her own battles. As for Naomi—*væ victis !* "

" If she be victimised ! " retorted Marcia, designedly avoiding the use of the less-galling verb " conquered."

" Pish ! " tossing his cigar-end over the rail,

like a naval captain going into action, and be-lieving the smoke would rise in volumes of another than nicotinic flavour. "It is a con-quest, and I'd have you to know that her father and my mother approve—"

"If you persist, Henry, we shall see what Naomi will do, with me at her side."

"If you oppose your mother's desire, you will act unlike her child."

"And if you proceed, you will be acting unlike your father's son."

Henry sprang up, overturning his chair, and so fiercely raised his hand, that Marcia's soul shrank, though her brave frame did not recoil an inch. He unclenched one finger of his fist, and pointing in-doors, hissed: "Leave me, girl, and be hanged to you!"

In the stamp of his foot, to emphasize the com-mand—though she had withdrawn at the words—was drowned the sigh of Mrs. Pleasanton, who, looking out of window, without being able to see the parties in the colloquy, whose angry tone had attracted her thither, had, at all events, distinctly caught the final sentences exchanged.

CHAPTER XVIII.

AFTER THE WOUND.

THE wound in her heart which Marcia received as she left her brother unnerved her, and she did not lift her head for nearly a week; but she continued sad—a sadness which time did not lessen. Observing her strange state, and knowing its cause, Henry did all he could to bring about a reconciliation. He treated her with unusual solicitude, which seemed to speak of repentance. He endeavoured to regain her affection, to disarm and appease her irritated pride. But he continued to perceive in her a cold repugnance, a gloomy reserve, which filled him with more dread than Cicely's menace inspired. He understood clearly that she had forgotten nothing, even if his cruel treatment had been forgiven in the brother, though never in the man.

At this juncture, Mr. Blandford, on the strength, ostensibly, of a few pleasant speeches exchanged with Colonel Pleasanton at the theatricals, paid a visit, and renewed it; but, though Mr. Pleasanton seemed to think his conversation would enliven Marcia, and so encouraged their being together, the young girl glided out of the snares easily, and threw the task of entertaining him upon her brother and mother. Mr. Rendall was busy at the Works.

One day, when she thus eluded the agent, and roamed the garden till she should see him walking to the station, she was startled to observe him on the wrong road, if that, as usual, were his destination. A curiosity, novel to her, impelled her to proceed to the same point of attraction. It was the cottage of Fordice. Mr. Blandford pitched on it with the precision of a man accustomed to solve more difficult problems, and disappeared within it from his watcher's view. That afternoon, followed by a servant with some eatables and brandy for the old workman, Marcia also paid him a visit. He was always garrulous towards her. She had no difficulty in ascertaining the inducement for the Londoner's stoop to a call on the cottage after his stay at the castle, so to put it.

" He's a vicious, sharp customer," observed Fordice, swallowing a little of the cognac presented to bathe his limb; for he wan't going to waste good liquor like that. " I've stopped the y'earth fur 'im, though. He was 'quiring about Elmwood—leastways, about the ruins there; and I 'lowed him to go away thinking the old family has died out—root, stock, and branch ! But I'm a wary old file—he! he! he! yes! old Fordice is;

and I could a' p'iuted out, not an 'underd mile fro'
this identicle place, the gentleman who owns the
name to the proputty. Catch me selling a real
gentleman to a varnished-up doll like him."

All this was so little satisfactory to Miss
Pleasanton, whose love of romance had anticipated a different result, that she refrained from
questioning, and dismissed Mr. Blandford as
clearly from her thoughts as she wished she could
do from her presence.   She returned to the house,
to confide her impression that the world was hollow,
and spun very creakingly upon its axis, to her
piano ; whereon Rendall, coming from the Works
fatigued, was astonished to hear her play something lugubrious.   He walked in and towards the
drawing-room, pushed open the door, and espied
her seated on her stool, weeping bitterly, with
her face hidden in her hands.

"What is the matter here ? " he cried.

Two or three sobs at first prevented Marcia
replying; then, drying her eyes with a sweep of
the back of her hand, as an untutored child may
do, she replied in a voice choking with tears :

"It is—ver—ver—very silly, but this piece of
Chopin's—the one he wrote as Mozart wrote his
requiem, for his funeral, you know—it always
cuts me up.   Papa will never allow me to play it.
But to-day, as no one was here, and I believed
you were at the Works, I thought I would bring
in a cry to relieve my feelings."

"You are naturally light-spirited, and this recent change in you comes from pain. Something has crossed the current in this family."

" No, nothing is the matter with me, I assure you, indeed and very deed ! If anything vexed me, I would tell you, of course ; and to-day I am not weeping, when papa promised me I should go up to town on Saturday morning to see the *matinée* of Reece's 'Haroun al Raschid,' at the Gaiety. I do so enjoy those nonsensical whimsicalities, do you not ? I hope they'll repeat that dance from ' La Girandole ' "—and she rattled off a lively dance tune. " Is it not like, in those bars, Pinsuti's Venetian Galley-slave's Song, which goes "—she played the two airs, one with each hand, to exhibit the resemblance. " Have you ever been there—to Venice, not the theatre ! Is it not singular that there should be a spot on the earth which one never saw out of photos and pictures, and yet which attracts one, and sets one dreaming about it ? For some it is one country ; for others a place widely different. As for me, I have never had a desire to see any place but Venice. I have always felt as though all musicians should die there, and be taken out on the lagoon in a gondola, and sunk in the sea, where the petrel should pipe and the briny breeze wail."

" The world is with you, and there is no necessity of their dying before they are doomed, for the rest of the ceremony to be expedited.'

She was deaf to his attempts to excite her smiles. She put her hands again on the keys, but she merely noiselessly skimmed over them, as though she were caressing the piano with the tips of her fingers ; then, allowing them to fall into her lap, she clasped them in a pensive attitude, and half turning her head towards the young professor, pursued :—

" Sadness, like electricity, I think, is in the air. There are days of moral sunshine, when you suffer from nothing, have no annoyances, no vexations ! You may wish to be sad then, you may even try back for gloomy ideas, and you cannot look blue ! I have often said I had a headache, and gone to lie down for nothing else but to have a good cry, with my head buried in the pillow, yet a fly in the pane has buzzed a comic tune, and I had to laugh. And at other times you feel too faint-hearted to resist the sadness that seems surcharging the air ; it will not be exorcised. It is like when you are beginning to swoon, delightful to feel your heart melt away ! "

" Morbid fancies ! This is not like you !" said Rendall. "I shall have your horse saddled, and we'll take a long ride ! "

" Not a bad idea !" jumping up. " And I warn you, I shall go like the wind ! "

CHAPTER XIX.

COLONEL PLEASANTON was laughing at a line in the list of guests at a reception in Downing Street.

"It is only Fitzbadger, who has gone over to swell the swell party at last," said he, with a reaction towards regret. "He will have to buy up any old files existent of the paper he established in '48, the *Libera Nos*; just as the tragic actress who began as a mythological divinity at the Royalty Theatre, seeks the photographs of her *Hesperida* to obliterate that record of her past. However, it's his granddaughter has worried him into surrender—she's so pretty and so eager to have a chance of captivating a title. It is natural."

"And quite right to put aside political nonsense when your children's future is at stake," said Mrs. Pleasanton.

"Just as we pocket a penknife found upon the table, when a child comes into the room," appended Rendall, who was breakfasting with them that morning, a month after the private theatricals.

"It's an old story that should be displaced by

a novelty," broke in Miss Pleasanton. " I am
sick and tired of hearing such an excuse for going
over to the enemy. I prefer those Jews of Jose-
phus who slew their families before they leaped
over the ramparts to die upon the Roman spears."

"He turned his coat for his wife and children's
sake, forsooth! One might as well say that all
children are good for is as cloaks for baseness. It
is as if being the father of a family gave a man the
right to be a scoundrel ! "

" Gently, my dear," said Mrs. Pleasanton.

" No, I am right; I know but two classes :
honourable folk, and the others. I am sure
my neighbour agrees with me."

" I ? not I," rejoined the professor. " I vote for
indulgences for the much married. I would have
them pensioned off, so much per infantine head.
The others, miserable, selfish bachelors, should be
sold as slaves, and not even allowed to wait
on their betters at official routs, levées, drawing-
rooms ! "

"I shall not talk to you any more," cried
Marcia, in an offended tone. " But, papa, I
cannot understand why this does not arouse
your indignation, for you always have sacrificed
everything to your opinions. What that rene-
gade has done is nauseating ! "

" I don't deny it ; but you are getting angry ;
and such occurrences are too common to waste
wrath upon."

"I should think I was firing up! and I'd like to fire down on such traitors! Look at the villain : he owed everything to forty years' abuse of all governments, and now he worships the stars he threw mud at. Your dear old friend Fitzbadger is a worthless wretch! "

"Tut, tut! my dear child; it is very easy to launch thunderbolts, but not at molehills, please. When you have lived a little longer you will be more indulgent. We must be more charitable, my child. You are too young in your feelings."

"No. This is not a question of youth, but of instinct. This runs in my blood—yours! I am too much of your daughter to mask my dislikes. It is an unprofitable temperament for this world if you will. But every time I see any one whom I know, or even don't know, sink below the standard of honour, my pain is too much for me; I feel as if I saw one of our swords turn into a snake, and turn, too, against my soldiers! It sickens me, it disgusts me, and I rush to grind it beneath the heel. And yet he will continue to expect you to respect him, will grasp your gallant hand. It is too much! I'm sure if ever he comes here, papa, I shall walk out past him with the regret I am not one of those gutter children to put out my tongue at his grandchild, which, I fancy, must be an intense gratification."

"The chocolate has made you too hot," observed the colonel smiling; "let me make you a 'snow-squall!'" by which he meant one of those "creations" in pounded ice, powdered sugar and milk, and lemon and sherry, which he had learnt to concoct in America. "That will cool you. As for putting out your tongue at people, that is too much in the daily movements of the snakes you loathed, and—but look at that political Viper gnawing a File in the collection of caricatures Mr. Pryse-Price sent down to your mother."

"Oh, I have not seen them!"

They rose from table, and Rendall brought her the album in the sitting-room.

Leaning over her father's shoulder as he turned the leaves, she looked at two or three pages, whereupon turning away her head she sighed: "That will do. Enough! Can there be any amusement in making people ugly, uglier than nature's freaks? What an idea! In the first place, in art, in books, in every thing, I am for the Beautiful. And distortions are not in the least entertaining. I should as soon laugh at a cripple. Do you like caricatures, Mr. Rendall?"

"No. Like monkeys, they make me deplore their uselessness. I put them away on the same shelf as my rough sketches of inventions, singular conglomerations found in a forgotten crucible, the joke books of the Brighton Pavilion, the paintings of Turner—"

"Oh, ——"

"And the songs of our music-halls."

"You are very kind," said Mr. Pleasanton, laughing ; "you are cutting my Gazette with a pencil-case, Rendall."

"Will you have a knife?" said Marcia, plunging her hand into her Gretchen satchel, whence she produced a heterogenous collection of things which she literally threw on the table.

"Tagrag and Bobtail!" exclaimed the professor. "Why, you carry a whole museum in your pocket! Work enough for a day for an auctioneer to sell off! What is it all ?"

"Presents, findings and pickings. So handy, as Mrs. Toodles says. There's the paper-knife you want," showing a "gem" to her father, before she handed it to Mr. Rendall. "You remember that you bought it for me, at Retford, when we were changing carriages. Oh, it is a long time ago. This," she took up another lethal instrument, "you brought me from the North. It has a German-silver blade, Swedish-iron springs, a bog-oak handle—I call it my international weapon. I gave you a George the Second penny for it, do you recollect ?"

"If we are going back to George the Second," said the Colonel "I must brush up my history."

"And what state papers are in that ?" asked the chemical expert, pointing to a small letter-case much worn, and pressed out with papers, the edges of which were yellow, frayed and dog-eared at the corners.

"My secrets!" Gathering up all the odds and ends she hastily put them in her *sac*, with the letter-case. Suddenly bursting into a fit of laughter, she dived again for the pocket-book, and opening the clasp, scattered on the table before the questioner all the slips it contained, and without opening them, referred to them one by one.

"That's the infallible gout prescription for papa, which made him worse—I put it by so it should not be made up again. That's a mess-room song he wrote for me about: 'The swords are only seven now, the bayonets seventeen!'—very touching; I began to set it to music."

"Come, come, put up your relics. You must no longer be so sentimental and romantic," said the colonel, prompted to the censure by a glance from his good lady, who came in at this nick. "Going down to the Works, Carroll?"

"Yes, colonel, I am getting on swiftly; broke the back of that obstinate amalgam yesterday— 212 degrees before it would move!"

"Let me go with you," cried Marcia. "I want to get some fresh ideas in colouration, and you have such pretty flames in your retorts."

"Flames and sparks!" cried the colonel, "There's nothing else in a young maid's fancy."

"In some fancies," said Rendall.

As the pair walked along, Marcia looked up from a rosebud she was opening, to study the folds, and asked,

"Am I really romantic, now? Do you rate me so?"

"Romantic? In the first place, what do you mean?"

"Oh, you know my meaning well enough. It is having ideas different to the common run. It is thinking of events which can never happen. For instance, a young lady is romantic when it grieves her to marry, as girls do marry, a gentleman in no way extraordinary; who enters quietly by the door, who is introduced to her by papa and mamma, and simply who has not saved her life the first time they met by stopping her runaway horse, or fishing her out of the water. You don't believe Miss Pleasanton is that sort of stuff, I hope?"

"No; at least I don't think anything at all about it. I'll engage you know nothing about it yourself."

"Your heroes of romance have never imposed on me. They are too well-bred, too handsome; overflow too profusely with agreeable qualities; unnatural, in short. There's an old chamber of horrors called the 'Mysteries of Paris'—ugh! but I rather lean towards the hero—a prince, who wears workman's clothes, and lives in a garret. Only, he does it for a disguise; whilst I should have accepted him as complete if he worked, as he pretended."

"There are different kinds of work Marcia.

o

Your prince would have earned half-a-crown a day as a bricklayer's man, and knocked his pretty hands to pieces; but he might have done very well as an engraver, a painter, or the like."

" He was something of that kind."

" Lord ' Jeames,' I dessay."

" You dare say nothing of the sort to a real prince like him. He could fence, and box, and shoot; though, after all, I have a sneaking sympathy for the roughs who rashly encounter these nonpareils; men who have been trained as gladiators; and, of course, easily overcome the brute who never could take out a gun-licence, and would use a foil to toast a herring upon."

" You fluctuate in your aversions like a woman. Your coming man is Apollo, master of all the arts; and, if Atlas gave him a hint, the use of the globes, and a fine bowman to boot, if you remember his serpent-slaying. As for the Marsyas case of cruelty, he was perhaps a creditor who would present his bill ; and even you do not pity a tradesman ' skinned ' alive by ' not-sufficient' cheques, do you ? "

" Well, I do not approve of you with your bitter jests. I never know when you are speaking with a thought of what you utter. I believe your lips often say things of their own accord. Now, I long for a good-natured gentleman."

" So you esteem good-nature ? "

" I do."

"And I also, Marcia, as one does a priceless valuable which is lost."

"You! but you are good-natured sometimes; lenient, at least."

"I am not vindictive, that's about all. I see revenge more agonising than I could inflict beset my foes. Perhaps I should be envious, if I had more modesty and less pride. But as for being good-natured, I have no time for benevolence. Age cures one of that as it does the hobbledehoy; a man grows out of his heart as he grows over the measles period."

"But grown people do have the measles. And you may yet be all kindliness."

"God grant it! That good-nature which sur-vives age and experience, the goodness which I have found in its virgin state in one or two men in the course of my life, is my idea of the best and most divine quality in our kind."

"But suppose this God-like gift abode in a mis-shapen shell—like those caricatures that so soon repelled me. Suppose your good-natured man, unlike Goldsmith's, was not young and handsome, and even superfine in attire and grace, but a Falstaff, a Deformed never to be Transformed, who dressed in a blue coat, flowered satin waistcoat, and trousers puffed out at the knee, and elephan-tine feet—how would you receive him, then?"

"I should be able, after the first glance, not to see his defects. Do I look at you, as we walk beside one another? But I know what you are like just as well as if my eyes were ever on you."

"But you ought to look at me now and then. If I were to attempt your likeness, I should not get the right hue of your eyes."

" Heart-colour."

" What ? "

" The colour of my heart appears in my eyes, when I look at you."

"What trifling ! we are debating gravely."

" Then let me say that, it being impossible for a woman to ignore the cut of a man's coat and the shape of his features, whatever his mental qualities, you cannot understand my welcome of the good-natured Caliban."

" But why should he not have a valet who would powder him up—"

" A man in powder, faugh ! "

" Marlborough went to battle powdered and patched like that columbine of ours ! "

" Ah, all men wore plaster and whiting in those days."

" And, then, why should not Good-nature go to a fashionable tailor? But you do not care for fashion or wealth. Father says you gave several discoveries to the public, that would have made fortunes."

"When I labour in private, my results are the public's. When I am employed—by your father, for instance, with his money, men, and appliances, the products are his, or in point of fact we arrange about the profits. If I wish for riches, it is that I may treat them as they deserve, to show the world how little respect I have for them."

" How ? "

"Possessing the unlimited circular note, I should roam the Continent till I met a Russian princess or an American girl—the two beings who can spend the most money in a given time. We should wed, and we should set to work dissipating our wealth. I despise the wealthy men whom people style extravagant, but who buy durable commodities : pictures, statues, palaces, yachts, diamonds, horses, theatres—they call that spending money ! I do not. It is investment, business, business. I should only buy the perishable, the intangible, give the waiters sovereigns, the Alpine guide a châlet and a herd, the glib-tongued monk who took me over a cathedral a canonry, the polylinguist who piloted me through Tunis his long red cap full of sequins ! and after a year of making innumerable little folk immensely blessed, I would send my wife home to the Susquehanna or Samovaria, as the case might be."

" Oh, what are you saying ? "

" An American or a Russian princess look at a poor man twice ? And I should wall myself up like an alchemist and pore over alembics till my eyes and powers failed me, and I fell into my furnace and was consumed like Empedocles in Etna."

"To prove you were a god?"

"To prove I was an ass, like the rest of my fellows."

"Well, yours are nice ideas! I must confess that I am no convert to your philosophy. A large fortune yields every *desideratum*—enjoyments, luxury, horses, carriages, painted silks, lace after your own designs, and the pleasure of plaguing fools and annihilating nuisances! I should submit to the affliction of being rich."

"I told you already, Marcia, you are a mere woman, nothing but a woman."

"A wummun?" echoed Fordice, standing at ease on his new crutches, to salute them as they passed his door; "don't he know an angel when he sees one? But he own'y says that to bank up his rale immotions—I know deeper nor that. They're sweet, one on t'other, they are. And if he knowed what I knows, there would not be so much slackness in his heart. He may thank me I nivor let the London chap get at him,—he'd pison him or anybody that stud between him and his gurl,— that's the quality of metal he is. I knows 'um well, them London fine-draw'd, cold-polished bits o' brass."

CHAPTER XX.

"WELL, there, I am heartily glad some one thinks the picture is worth the money;" said Mr. Millward, as he showed Rendall the portrait of Cicely in her dress in "One Fool makes Many." "I cannot see the likeness, though the dress looks the thing. A thousand and fifty pounds is a pull for two months' painting. But that man Milletone is dead-set against capital, like the rest of his tribe. Miss O'Rotunda's was, if anything, larger, and very much less. Because he is an artist he has no fixed price, no tariff, a right to fleece me! As for that, it is our bad English habit to charge according to the purchaser's position. If a working man asks another the nearest public-house, he is answered without the hand being held out; but if I inquire for a number, the man says, ' That's thirty-two, sir—got a shillin', m' lord?' And his secretary —these painting men have secretaries now!—wrote me so sharp a letter: if Cicely did not begin her sittings on such and such a date, Mr. Milletone could not receive her for another six weeks! Civil enough, but it was 'take it or leave it,' without the monogram and the flummery."

"Very true," answered the professor, in his

soberest professional tone; "quite right, artists profit by their reputation."

Millward and his daughter were dining at Gratchley this evening. The marriage of Henry Pleasanton with Naomi was an understood bargain. The colonel had been won over, we mean talked over, if not dazed by the glitter of gold. This severe, rigid, incorruptible, upright blade of war, had insensibly allowed the Millwards' immense fortune to weigh on his thoughts, impose upon his dreams, approach his pickets, and parley with them over temptations. He was deluded, and then disarmed. For his son, since the success of his scheming, he had begun to feel that respect which one conceives for a capacity which finally asserts its power, or a fortune which reveals its greatness. Moreover, he thought Henry a marvel of abnegation because he took the younger girl for her sweetness, and had not sought the heiress, her sister; for the colonel knew nothing of the secret between his wife and Mr. Blandford.

Marcia, who for some time had been fretting thoughtfully, was almost cheerful again this evening. She amused herself by naming " Rich man, poor man, beggarman, thief" the turquoises on Naomi's necklace in three rows, while the latter, indolent and absorbed, her eyes cast down, replied in monosyllables to Mrs. Pryse-Price's interminable chatter, and only roused herself when Mr. Rendall's caustic sallies were audible.

"Nowadays," went on Mr. Millward, "the co-operation idea is playing the very mischief. And then the holding-back-rent doctrine has begun to fructify in England. In the West one of my agents excuses his low receipts on that score. Personally, I care little "—he meant individually—" for England will last my time. But in 1900—"

"What are you saying, Mr. Millward?" inquired the colonel, joining the speaker and his chemical adviser.

"Only that I fear our children will come to want bread some day."

"Why, you'll frighten them from going into matrimony," returned the veteran, plying a gold toothpick.

"Oh, don't let papa fall into one of his gloomy fits of foreboding! If once he begins to talk of the end of the world, it is as dull as a Handel festival," said Miss Millward.

"I am glad my girls do not share my fears," said the capitalist; "but we have had a calm too long; all our wars will not be perpetually abroad against the nigger, yellow, red, or black. We have to fight the white slaves at home."

"Better flog some of those grinding middlemen," interrupted Miss Millward. "I read that the seamstresses are paid only a couple of shillings for an ulster; and merely to make a few flimsy alterations in mine. Madame Dodolphine wrote two guineas in the bill. To be sure, mine was all hand-work — one must encourage manual labour—and the material silver-fox and plush— but the proportion would be the same."

" But it is only in France they have revolutions every leap-year," said Mrs. Pleasanton.

" Quite so," took up Mr. Rendall. " The English are too fond of their beef, and bread, and beer—"

" The three B's," interpolated Mr. Millward, as one who said a neat epigram, and he received the conventional reward in the smile awaiting a joke with invisible point.

" The generals of our mobs, so far," proceeded the young professor, " are incompetent. Now, if I had the post of Commander-in-Chief of the mob—in 1900, always understood—I should act very differently."

" Or indifferently, as you did as prompter," said Marcia.

" Oh, you are there, are you? I should lead my horde straight out of their alleys into the West-end, so that the house owners would implore the military not to employ cannon, lest they injured their statues by Tabagghi, and their daughters' portraits by Milletone. Then, having plundered the gin-shops and provision stores, and emptied all the liquor into the Thames, which should run brandy-and-water that day, I should lodge in the ten-thousand-pounders, run the plate into bullets, and hold out, house by house, as a fort, till we were overcome, or the country rose to our aid. After our defeat, if that came, there would be plenty of work replacing the property we had consumed; and lovers of the poor, like Mr. Henry Pleasanton, would immortalise me in 1920 or so."

" But, at present," said the statistician referred to, " we are too prosperous below the upper classes for active discontent, too fond of material comfort. If the working-man should fight now, it would not be for abstract ideas, but for a better coat, a silk hat a sealskin jacket for his daughter, a trap to put his donkey to—"

" That is why I should lead my army directly into the quarter where good things are stored," remarked Rendall. " You see I admit all your figures. The life of the people has been lengthened, and they eat more—beans ! and more—American bacon ! but is this any reason why you should believe in the immortality of the actual constitution of society ? Revolutions form a cycle, but, unfortunately for Mr. Millward, no one has calculated the times of reappearances. Say 1900, and let us go on at the jog-trot till we see the vanguard from St. George's-in-the-East passing St. James's, Piccadilly. I shall have made diamonds a drug in the market before then !"

" Oh, what a shocking intention !" exclaimed

Miss Millward, taking a dislike to the stone from that moment, impressed by the sincere conviction of the speaker.

"I am selfish," said her father; "and, after all, there is one consolation, the fools do not think money so much an enemy as aristocracy."

"You are right, sir," answered Rendall. "But I, in 1900, should sack the Bank and Cheapside on the march to the Albert Memorial. I have two cartridges ready—one to blow up the walls, and the other to extinguish any flames and lay the dust—every chemist knows them—so that my lieutenants would be packing up the scattered gold in half an hour after the beadle descended from a trip through Saturn's ring upon the ruins. It is the Exchange that is the community's enemy, Crockford's writ large."

"I have had a circular from a stockbroker: you can send in stamps on sheets, like the Post Office Savings-bank schemes, till a pound accumulates, and then he will invest for you. Even the office-boy can speculate as easily as he can bet." So spoke Mr. Pleasanton the minor.

"The peerage is the head," went on the professor, "and it will lose life speedily enough if the heart is rent asunder. And the heart is money."

"Oh, you don't know anything about the heart!" cried Marcia, tartly.

Naomi sighed audibly, so that all looked at her, and, as she blushed, laughed long and loud.

CHAPTER XXI.

THE GOLDEN BALL.

THERE was a large party at Millward Hall,
for they wished to do honour by a grand ball
to the approaching espousal of Naomi to Mr.
Henry Pleasanton, it being understood that the
marriage would not take place until, at least, the
elder daughter should also be formally engaged.

"You are in great spirits. How often you
dance!" said Marcia to Naomi, as she fanned her
in a corner of the spacious drawing-room.

" I never danced so much certainly." She took
her by the cord of her fan, and led her into an
adjoining room. There she kissed her, saying:
"Oh, how delightful it is to feel happy!" and
kissing her again, after this truism, in a transport
of joy, she whispered to her : " *She* loves *him*
no more, if ever she did ! I am very sure. I was
altogether mistaken in my reading of their conduct,
in my ignorance; for lately, since I have studied
how Cicely behaves towards one whom she favours
with confidences — towards Mr. Rendall, for an
example—I am certain that your brother Henry
was not beloved."

"Does she regard our bitter-cup, Mr. Rendall, very tenderly, then, but without any real lifting up of her heart towards him?" queried Marcia, sternly. "She must not flirt with him. He almost lives in our house,—he is like a brother; and I will not allow him to be coquetted with."

"Oh, a chemist!"

"An alchemist, darling! a light of science! I cannot value him properly, for he never talks such things to me. I wish he would. But you should see the men at the works! They idolize him, and walk in terror of his knowledge. If a man has a spark in the eye, a scald, a palsy from standing in the air-blast after stoking, well, upon my word, he is a magician; he beckons the splinter of iron out of the eye, he runs his hand over the scald, and it is soothed, he stirs a glass of water with his pencil-case, and lo! the sufferer is strong again. No, Cicely is tremendously lovely, but she must not think to twist such steel round her finger—it won't 'stay;'—he is not a ribbon-snake, our Mr. Rendall, but an anaconda; and when it comes to twisting round any one, he'd squeeze them to death! My father says he is a chip of the old block, and he knew his father once, a very devil incarnate when roused. But you are happy! never mind your sister. Happy because you love *him* now?"

Naomi stopped her own mouth, by gently pressing her bouquet to her lips.

"Oh, have I found you, Miss Pleasanton? you promised me the 'Bostonian.'" With which address, Mr. Blandford carried off Marcia from Naomi, who, as she passed along, blew her a grateful kiss.

Naomi's confession had caused Marcia a thrill of joy. Though she loved her brother no more, her mother would be happy and content. Suddenly a recollection returned to her to cause uneasy thought and vague terror : the certainly improving friendship of Cicely and Carroll. But now she ought to see nothing dark on the horizon, nothing threatening in the future. Dismissing the foreboding of an evil, for it loomed up like one, she went through the dance quite gaily, and was taken to a chair.

"Well, Mr. Blandford, am I very much dishevelled? You look at me very hard, I must exclaim."

The agent's partner wore a cream-white brocade gown, garlanded with ivy leaves in gold, *mat* with the ribs burnished, and small red berries, which also extended to the body of the dress and to the puff at the shoulder, like the ladies of the Emperor Maximilian's court. A long wreath of ivy, with the same red berries, was entwined in her hair, its ends trailing on her shoulders to a necklace of gold medallions bearing each an emerald, a Brazilian jewel of her father's gift.

She sat with her head stiff on the sofa. Her beautiful wavy hair, brushed to the front.

encircled the upper part of her bright forehead. A
tender, deep, and gentle light escaped from her
brown, swimming eyes. The light played on her
cheeks. The shadow hovered round the corners
of her mouth ; and her lips, which were usually
closed in a slightly contemptuous pout, were now
relaxed and half open in self-felicitation. She
was charming above most women there, thought
Blandford. The outline of her face disappeared in
her childish happiness, as in an Asiatic sun.

"You are full of smiles this evening, Miss
Pleasanton."

" Not only on this evening, I hope."

" Nor for this evening, *I* hope ! I will tell you
frankly that when I had the honour of making
your acquaintance at your house, you wore such a
saddened look. Joy becomes you much better."

" Do you think so ? How do I waltz ? "

" Worthy a choicer cavalier. I keep bad time.
That's why you refused me another spin."

" Did I ? There's absenteeism for you ! No,
no, absence of mind. I am full of political
phrases from that brother of mine. I have an
unconquerable inclination for dancing this evening, and so we shall have time enough. Oh,
don't refer to your watch ; I don't want to know
the exact hour ! But you must not think me
exhilarated by dancing ! No, I am happy—
very happy. I wish I could cement my new
bond with Fortune with a triple, a tenfold seal

Do you game—play cards? I mean, are you superstitious?"

"Really, I—"

"Of course you are!"

"I am afraid I believe in nothing, except the goodness of fair women."

"I should like to give away my odd silver to the first half dozen beggars I met, as I have heard say gamblers do when they leave their club with winnings."

"It is a fad; a habit. I shall be happy to be your almoner—plenty of beggars round Victoria or Charing Cross—if it will continue your happiness," said Blandford.

"Oh, do not take all I say in earnest. But we must not dance twice consecutively. I mean to dance every number, so you may have a renewal of your annoyance later on. Mr. Pryse-Price, pray, let me have your arm."

Blandford waited where he was till he caught the eye of the heiress. He gave her a look which sufficiently revealed that they had intimately conferred before that hour, and Cicely, in a magnificence that made the very mirrors blink, swooped down upon the agent.

"Miss Millward," said he, with a bow a great deal more respectful than his tone, "there is no opposition in the Pleasanton family now. The young lady who has a temper of her own that might have made trouble, has been made sweet."

"Nevertheless, that marriage must not come off."

"It is a pity, too, that Miss Pleasanton was not still in the opposition, for I had a vague notion that her friendship with that celebrated chemist might lead to a pretty little dose of poison which leaves no traces in the cup of—"

"Go on. I am listening, sir." Her face wore a set smile, in which her lips, marble white from the firm drawing back, resembled those of the caryatid behind her, which held the electric globe inundating the pair.

"Would you prevent the marriage by the delay through illness—more or less speedily fatal—of your sister or Mr. Pleasanton?"

"Naomi? No, no. Such as she never offend me. But he—if no other way presents itself—let him die, Mr. Blandford. I say, clearly, let him die. He has insulted me beyond reparation."

She glided away, and, superbly condescending, took the place for the time of a lady withdrawing from a set in order to get a trailing lace flounce set to rights. Then returning, she added, with more emotion than she had pronounced the death sentence :

"Have you a complete book upon Mr. Rendall? What are his prospects, his standing, his family?"

"Don't know too much. I found an old stubborn dolt who lived where he was born, on his father's land—all sold now, bv the way—but the brute is invulnerably dense. He is not to be sounded."

"But every man has a father, mother, relations?"

"No; his is a turbulent lot. The pedigree reads like a battle roll. I wonder he has not been knocked over the head at five-and-twenty like the rest; or, perhaps, the average is thirty; just his age, so there is hope yet. And, another perhaps, he is to perish from a wound in the heart, 'a dart of Miss Millward's eyes.' How splendid you are! No wonder the old Earl of Fairfield, who merely came down to look in, went away grieving that he must keep good hours."

"Could *I* marry him?"

"If you let him go, find a gold mine somewhere first. It is in his business to handle the divining rod. Before you let *me* go—how about the title for Mr. Pleasanton—"

"A collar for the dead dog?"

Blandford caught his chin between finger and thumb, like Fleury's "Cellini reflecting."

"I see a chance of making some money; and since your father is in the vein to squander his wealth, why not Mr. Blandford the gainer?"

"Father has been promised the baronetcy for whom he wills."

"Then he will be buying land then? Why not this dead bit which I came across by Elmwood?"

He was talking to himself, for the lady had swept

away.   " The   Wightwardens owned it twenty
years ago.   It may rouse up that brood.   Nothing
like claiming land dormant to awaken heirs.   But
it is time I reminded Miss Pleasanton of her
promise."

CHAPTER XXII.

ASHAMED OF HIS NAME.

I HARDLY know whether even to think of spending the evening with you again," said Rendall to Miss Pleasanton, as she intercepted him on the road from the Works. "Your mother was in a very bad temper, sour towards me when not sullen, after the ball at Millward's."

"It is not at you, conceited donkey; at me. You can venture to-night, for they are as jolly as sandboys."

"But why at you? I believe it is thanks to you Naomi accepted Henry, and even persuades herself she loves him.'

"So she does, truly. They were vexed at me— mamma really, papa only enough to keep countenance with her—because I jilted another pretender to my hand."

"Another? You are a pluralist in matrimonial propositions."

"Pooh! this is only the fourteenth. I am not acquiring the knack of letting them down lightly. This time *you* were the cause of it."

"Indeed! How was that?"

Marcia buried her hands in her ulster pockets, and began stepping off briskly. Then turning, with an attempt at a whistle, she said, taking his hand upon her arm, as if she were the cavalier :

" Yes, you, old friend! you do not like the man. Mamma had it cut and dried; Henry nodded with approval; Papa nodded with sleepiness ; and you were not by. But your influence never leaves me when I have need to do a wise thing."

" Thank you, *sir*," piped the professor in falsetto.

" So much money! Henry said he was astonished, but Mr. Millward attested the figures. I was tormented the whole day. And then I reflected duly. I slept very badly for over two nights. How can a miser repose on his treasure? It was papa I thought of in this proposal. Would he not be proud? That is the point. He is proud of me as it is ; but as wife of a man noted in London,—you should see the Duke of Diamonds talk with him at the ball, like an elder brother! But your principles came into my mind. Your ideas, your paradoxical theories, all sorts of things you have said to me. I thought of your contempt for mere money, that decided me,—for gains made upon secrets, hush-money, in short; and he was not a silly, brainless courtier this time, my man very different from Goddard, and that crew. Imagine his saying to me : ' Miss Pleasanton, I am well aware that I do not over-please you ; but

allow me to hope that, after a time, I shall dis-
please you a little less.' He was quite affecting;
the true ring in his tone, but not the wedding
ring. A good comedian—we missed a valuable
assistant for our play. I was on the point of
saying: 'Suppose we mingle our tears together?' Fortunately, when I was inclined to
grieve, papa, on the other hand, gave me a desire
to laugh, with a tragi-comic face. Dear papa!
half-gay, half-sad. I never saw resignation so
jolly or happiness so resigned! Sorrow at losing
me, and joy at seeing me make a good match.
But it blew over! Papa gave me a reproving
look, when mamma was eyeing us, but not in
earnest. He was relieved in his heart. But
come in. It is a silver-sea now."

"You have not mentioned the gentleman's
name," remarked Rendall, who had patiently let
the rigmarole be uncoiled.

"Did I not?—Mr. Blandford."

"So he hovered round here to pay his *devoirs*
to you?" he queried, with a glow of indignation.
"He is very cunning to conceal the first moves so
well, under an opening which beseemed another
game. You may as well tell Mr. Blandford that
the men, who saw him pay a visit to old Fordice's
cottage, took it into their heads that he was
fishing for a factory secret,—trying to peep
into my laboratory after hours; and he may get
soused in the tempering-trough."

"I saw him—" But there she stopped in her revelation of having dogged the agent. "I mean there is no fear of that. He will never see me again."

"That is well. Such men are like those venomous spiders, each of whose feet are a poison-fang; though they may have no intention to sting, they leave a searing trace on the innocent flesh over which they have crawled."

Marcia shuddered; her flesh crept in sympathy with the illustration. But, as the next moment they entered the house, and the absurd discord of the colonel attempting "Lochaber no more" on the black keys with one finger, met their ears, she laughed, and went into the drawing-room laughing.

A look of happiness was on every countenance. The colonel's good humour shone mischievously in his eyes. His wife's countenance expressed quiet satisfaction. Flying into the room in her childish joy, Marcia supercharged it with the lively movements, almost the flutter of birds' wings.

"About time you looked in again!" hailed Colonel Pleasanton.

"I thought," said the lady to her daughter, "that you would bring Henry back from the station."

"Why, he said he will not be down again till the day after to-morrow; then, without fail."

"How good of you to come!" proceeded the colonel. "We must try to make up to you for the pleasures of Millward Hall, of which you are depriving yourself."

As he shook hands with Rendall, he winked at his wife, as a cue.

"Yes, yes! Come here a moment, Mr. Rendall," said the lady. "I must know if you have discovered the water of eternal youth! Not that I mean to imply Miss Millward will stand in need of a draught for years; but—"

"Gammon!" broke in the colonel. "He goes to play billiards with her father! he's such a splendid player! Ha! ha! ha!" laughing till he was purple, and the scars on his face gleamed white.

"Undoubtedly, Miss Mill—"

But they let him get no farther.

"Undoubtedly, you are a 'fraud,' as they say over the water!" cried the colonel. "Never you mind Mrs. Pleasanton. She is in a merry mood to-night, and so am I, and—"

"So say all of us!" said Marcia; but her accent was not at the hilarious pitch of the others.

"But, in billiards or flirtation, I say, 'Go in and win!'" slapping Rendall on the shoulder, as he gave him a chair near him.

"No," intervened Marcia. "Give me up my sworn tormentor, or I shall go and play the 'Big Bashaw's March' till you are deafened."

"Does he not keep his coolness capitally?" said the colonel, and then followed such laughter as old ladies indulge in who have been entertaining themselves with a racy bit of scandal.

"How heartfree you all are!" Rendall could not help uttering, sarcastically; for all this merriment, just after Marcia's escape from a man like Blandford, made his blood run cold.

"As merry as grigs!" cried Marcia. "This is our future style: we shall be as merry as this to-morrow, and next day, and so on, shan't we, papa?"

"My darling!" said the colonel, as she came near him, to draw the professor away, and he detained her, "you are beside me, as I remember you and Henry when I came came back from those wars among the 'greasers.' You were most like the boy then, with your hair cut short and curling crisply. You ran your fingers over these scars and said, 'Oh, papa, you are not like other gentlemen!' but you said, thoughtfully, 'I should not like my papa to be like other gentlemen!' It is such sayings on the spur of the moment which recompense one for the pain and trouble you give us parents. A family is a heavenly compensation, Carroll, nothing like children to twine round a heart."

"You are making him dull, papa; these bachelors do not like pap to be served them. He would rather have my piano than a baby's rattle. Come,

he shan't talk nursery, a naughty, fond *pater!*
Cheer up! be brilliant! You don't sparkle in
the least."

"Something is the matter with you, Mr. Rendall," said her mother.

"Nothing at all," was the reply. "I may be a
little tired. I have been chasing a combination
for a week—a combination that will not come."

"Well, sir; you make haste and be free.
You shall invent me some combination that will
startle them as a bridesmaid's dress. We mean
to have a show-wedding, a banquet here; the
house thrown into the grounds, bands a-blowing,
and wine a-flowing. I shall make you tipsy,
Carroll!" using his Christian name for the first
time before her parents. "Then you will be
lively, if you are glum now. You are not
half a companion. Heigho! I wish Naomi
were here. Has she not even written to me?"

"No. She sent over a newspaper," replied
Mrs. Pleasanton. "It was half out of the
wrapper, so I took the liberty of opening it."

"What has she marked?" cried Marcia.

"Those newspaper fellows have not got hold
of the marriage, have they?" growled the colonel,
with a soldierly abhorrence of the pen.

"No, papa; it's only a reference to our theatricals, and a hope such a talented company will
repeat the pleasant programme this winter. See,
Mr. Rendall, not a word about the prompter,

'whom we saw not at all and heard too often!'

Rendall took the paper mechanically, but with that vagary of the sight which will look obliquely sometimes, his eyes skipped the paragraph framed in an inky line, and read this one instead:

"Our readers who failed to notice in the *Times* of yesterday an advertisement concerning change of name, will thank us for repeating the gist of it. It is to the effect that Mr. Henry Pleasanton, of Gratchley House, only son of the gallant proprietor of the Works there, has commenced the formalities by which he will be known, after the requisite period, as Henry Wightwarden, Esq., from the name of the property he has acquired near Elmwood, in Lincolnshire."

He mastered the feelings induced by this announcement, and pushed the paper aside with so much parade of its being worthless that when Marcia asked after it next morning, she suspected not in the slig htest degree that he had picked it upon the first opportunity and put it in his pocket for destruction at his leisure.

That night Mrs. Pleasanton woke up her husband. There was a glare of light on the ceiling. But on going downstairs and getting his field-glasses, he was able to reassure her.

"The Works are quite safe. It is only the cottage of old Fordice. Job tells me that he went up to town at eight o'clock, so there's no loss of life; and I was thinking of housing him better."

CHAPTER XXIII.

THE DEVIL ON TWO STICKS.

THE name of the property which Henry Pleasanton had added to his patronymic, with a view to be ennobled upon its base, happened to be, by a singular but not unexampled coincidence (he thought, not being in Mr. Blandford's confidence), the name of a manorial estate in Lincolnshire, and of a family formerly illustrious, but so lost sight of in the present day that everyone believed it was extinct. The latest member of historical note died in Belgium, after the battle of Ligny His son married early, but died on the Continent. His four children, all boys, seemed accursed, for everything went wrong in their hands; two drank themselves to death, one committed a homicide, and though thought to have fled during a dozen years, was found in a pond where he had expiated his crime; the last, utterly impoverished by paternal law costs, went abroad, and worked as a common labourer in the Almeida quicksilver mines, resisting the baleful fumes with rare success; afterwards he worked in America. He returned to England, changed, unknown, and was taken on at Gratchley Works. When Mr. Rendall came there, he was opposed by the workmen, who detested him for proposing innovations. The last of the Wightwardens, however, shielded Carroll, telling his mates "straight" that they were wrong, that this Englishman was preferable to a German, Belgian, or Swiss, and even resorting to blows when words were valueless. It was pure manliness to befriend the lone youth against a herd, for it was not till Blandford came to Fordice's cottage and exhibited certain papers that Fordice, or Wightwarden, learnt that he had a son living in the chemical expert.

On the same day as Carroll, the old workman had seen the local paper and read that paragraph concerning Mr. Henry Pleasanton. Since his discovery that he had a son alive, and a worthy man loving a girl as desirable as Marcia, old Fordice had changed, becoming less irascible, untameable and bearlike. But, nevertheless, the turbulent spirit of his race, which had made it dreaded in the Wars of the Roses, and the time of Cromwell, boiled up, and he arrived in London that night as furious as a baited bull.

He meant to have annihilated the usurper on the spot. But once in town, in crowded streets of glaring shops, the stream of life and motion, noise and confusion, filled him with the bewilderment of the wild beast let loose in the amphitheatre, whose rage is daunted, and who stops short after

his first plunge. He spent a sleepless night at a
coffee house, and went next morning to the cham·
bers of a legal firm of which he remembered both
name and address, and which had drained his
father of a small fortune. The house was there,
the name still up; but the firm was represented by
a lawyer who had purchased the business, a cool,
polite, white-headed man, who, wheeling round in
a green morocco arm-chair, with eyes half closed,
listened to his whole business, his title, his rights,
his indignation, the crackling of old parchments
which he was turning over with a trembling hand.
His listener's countenance remained perfectly im-
moved. When Mr. Raymond Wightwarden had
done, he feared he had not been heard, and was
about to begin again. But the solicitor stopped
him with a finger up, saying :

"You will gain your suit, I think."

"What, you think I will! not sure?"

'A law suit is always a lottery, sir," replied
the other, with such an extremely doubtful smile
that it froze the hearer, ready to fly into a passion.
"But all the chances are in your favour; and
I am ready to undertake the business for a son
of an old client of my predecessors."

"Here, then," said the rough client, placing his
bundle of proofs on the table; "I'll thank you to
take it up forthwith, sir."

"One moment, Mr. Wightwarden," said the
solicitor, on seeing him move towards the door.

"I have to remark that in a matter of this sort, an important case that will probably only be finally settled in the House of Lords, for the Fairfields are well known—I have had her ladyship the countess, a very famous beauty, in this office, sir!—there are preliminary expenses, registries to be examined, extracts from records to be made. I am obliged, therefore, to ask you to cover me in these outlays, if you wish me to undertake your suit. If I may draw on your banker for five hundred pounds, say as a beginning—"

"Five hundred devils!" cried the client, more like the workman than the noble, crimsoning. "My name is stolen from me, and because I did not know a man was going to rob me, I must pay five hundred pounds to make that rascal give me back my name! Five hundred pounds! I told you, Mr. Chafferwell, very clearly, that I have been nothing but a common hammerman and plain-moulder for years. It is true my son is better off; but no! I would rather have presented him with his own right clear, when I told him who he was. Sir, I have no such sum."

The solicitor pulled up his collar tips, after the fashion of a counsel hitching up his gown, which is the Anglo-legal gesture, instead of a shrug *more Gallice*, and replied :

"I regret exceedingly, Mr. Wightwarden; but

the formalities are indispensable. You must have little difficulty in procuring the money, for families to which yours has been allied would back you up immediately. The Fairfields are very rich, for one. Besides, a family league should always support a claimant in such matters."

"Sir, I know no one; and the last Wightwarden will ask no one. Since law is not for me, I will rely in the justice which abides in my right hand, though my leg is hardly well, and wants the strength the arms still have. But you might let me look at the directory I saw in your outer office."

"Oh, Fairfield House is—"

"I am not wishful to see a lady; I am going to confront the thief who has stolen my title."

And copying out the address of Mr. Henry Pleasanton, he departed from the solicitor's office.

Mr. Goddard was seated smoking and drinking with Mr. Henry Pleasanton-Wightwarden, as he began to sign himself, in an interregnum, after which the Pleasanton should be dropped. Mr. Goddard had not cherished the slightest grudge because his companion's sister had thrown him over.

"I came down on my feet, as I generally do; no harm done, dear old chappie."

So they were smoking and talking by the fire, when they heard a noise, a parley and scuffle in

the outer room; and almost immediately the door
burst open, and a sturdy man on crutches entered
quickly, hurling aside the servant, though a stout
varlet, who wished to bar his passage.

"So I see Mr. Henry Pleasanton," began he.

"What's the meaning of this?" cried Henry,
rising.

"Who begins to call himself 'Wightwarden'?"

"Why, it is Fordice, one of my father's men,
drunk or cranky." Henry muttered explanatorily
to Goddard. "What the devil is the meaning of
your storming in here? Come, Fordice, this sort
of thing won't do! 'tis not the way to get a pass
for a hospital, if that's—"

"You are speaking to Raymond Wightwarden,
the Fairfield Wightwardens!" returned the man on
crutches, approaching the table, and neither bearing himself nor speaking in a way that contro-
verted his sudden pretensions to be something
more than ever his mates had suspected. "And
you are a thief whom I do the honour of address-
ing."

"A thief!" murmured the blanched lips of Henry
Pleasanton. "Take care what you are saying—"

"Take care what you are doing, thief! Thief,
for you have stolen my name!"

Letting his crutches fall, by some miracle of
hatred and indignation and exorbitant pride of race,
Raymond Wightwarden leaned over the table, supported on his right hand, and with the sinister

intention of using only the less honourable hand,
smote Pleasanton on the cheek with the left, so
that the young man's teeth rattled. The one who
was struck staggered back with an "Oh!" in
nothing but pain. He recovered his balance, and
waving aside Goddard, who had plucked up a spirit
on the ruffian letting the formidable crutches fall,
he coolly folded his arms, and said, in his calmest
voice :

"I believe I understand you, sir. You think
there is one Wightwarden too many. So do I."

The intruder gave a surprised growl of delight.
He knew the young man so long that he had
never imagined such a speech would come from
his lips even when struck.

"Leave your address with my man. My
solicitor will confer with yours on the matter of
the name, which belongs to the property I bought.
You see, I do you the honour to believe you are
misled. After we have fought that out in the
courts, I will settle with you for this brutal
assault. It looks as if some enemy had planned
a scandal." He had Miss Millward in his mind.
"But your principal is foiled ; I will not have
it said that I locked up the man who disputed
a title-deed with me in order to prejudice his
claim."

"What!" ejaculated the rough visitor, red as
the flannel shirt peeping from under his grey
woollen one. "Is there no fight in you? As I

thought. Law-courts! Don't you understand
that I mean fight?"

"This is not a fighting country, sir," replied
Henry, quietly. He nodded for the servant to
remove his unwelcome visitor, but the man showed
no eagerness to approach the devil on two sticks.
"And besides," seeing that Goddard frowned a
little, and drew away slightly at this, he added,
"if it were, I cannot have to do with a working-
man, an old man, and a cripple."

"Thief and coward!" said Fordice. "When
my father found the white liver in a dog, he did
not merely thrash him—as I would otherwise do
to you when my bones are healed—but shoot him.
But you shall have no excuse. I have a son—a
son, sir; and he shall contest your right to steal
our name."

Grinding his teeth to overcome a spasm of pain,
he limped to the door with the heavy, slow beat
of his crutches, sounding in the young man's ear
like the step of the statue in the ears of Don
Giovanni.

"A bear!" cried Henry, whisking out his
scented handkerchief and wiping his face. "What
a brute! George!" He called to his servant,
"Water. After all, it is a blessed thing he struck
low: I may have to see Mr. Wrench, but I shall not
have a black eye. It would have been devilish
awkward, for we are going over to Calais in Millward's yacht for the banquet of the Tunnel Com-

pany and the ball in the Casino. Do you not go?"

"I had an invitation," returned Goddard, debating inwardly whether he should get an "opinion" of the club committee on the possibility of his associating with the speaker hereafter.

"Then you are sure to go. I never saw Miss Millward in fairer trim. Goddard, dear chummie, why don't you make up to that charming inheritor of Babbage alone-can-calculate how many thousands a year."

It was an idea. The saturnine young gentleman concluded he would not cut his friend just yet.

"Besides, I wish to keep out of my father's way, and that will be an excuse. He doesn't stomach my change of name either." He recalled Marcia's outbreak, which confirmed his surmise. "Are you going to the club? I wish to look in at Blandford's."

CHAPTER XXIV.

THROWN AT HIS HEAD.

MR. MILLWARD'S yacht "Conquistador" was one of the largest afloat, and more expensively furnished than any other. Cicely had designed the porcelain panels and plaques in the sitting-room after the Vatican arabesques, and they did credit, said Blandford, to her hand and her father's purse.

The French side of the Channel Tunnel had advanced another thousand inches, and the Company gave a celebration. Millward was interested, and proposed to make it quite an excursion. The Pleasantons would have all gone, but at the last moment the colonel's wife was afraid of the sea, and her daughter staying to nurse her, and the colonel to guard them, there having been a raid of burglars at a village near Millward Hall, neither of the ladies were on the steamer. Mr. Rendall, at the instance of Marcia, who said his remaining "as well" would look bad, together with her mother remaining ashore "as ill," shook off a disinclination and sailed.

It was an indescribable surprise of a night the :

smooth face of the sea shining with silvery moon-
light. All the ladies were on deck, in wraps it
is true, but laughing at the idea of their being
chilly. Henry Pleasanton and Goddard, who
were closer "chums" than ever of late, were
together. Mr. Blandford was watching Cicely,
who had played a "Hymn to the Sea" of some
Italian master, on an American organ, to the
pleasure of fishermen drifting on the calm surface.
The music over, she circled among the guests,
like a hawk picking out a plump chicken in the
hennery, and secured Mr. Rendall.

"You are not in your element this night," she
said, burying her chin in her fleecy shawl. "Not
fond of the sea ? "

"I believe my father was lost upon it in the
Bay of Biscay ; anyway, I never care for it.
The shorter the voyage the happier I. But I feel
dull to-night. Your playing had too many deep
notes." He preferred Marcia's marches and
American dances to Cicely's ultra-high art.

"You are a man of mystery," she said mean-
ingly. "This is the first time I ever heard the
gentleman cited, and not even now by name."

"Never, perhaps. My mother was exaggeratedly
proud. Being poor, she gave up her marital
name, and took another, under which I have
passed."

"It little matters, sir. You are the man to
make a name," said Cicely, tenderly "Leave it

to nonentities like Henry Pleasanton to borrow those of others."

" You do not like him. That is awkward, when he enters your family."

"Oh, any one enters a rich man's family. Gilded doors are easily forced. I shall marry some building contractor, steamship owner, great farm proprietor in the West of America, or the like. I did dream of a nobleman once, but Beauty is the craze. The Earl of Fairfield wedded a barmaid, or no better, simply for her looks."

"She is exhaling bitterness," remarked Blandford to Major Bouncable. "She smiles so much. Let us go and inhale bitter beer."

The moment the agent's eye was off her, Miss Millward seemed to breathe more easily

" My father tells me you cold-shoulder his propositions to leave Gratchley Why not tell him your terms ? "

" I am happy there."

" But the home will be broken up. The son marries, and, I am pretty sure Naomi will go to a warmer clime. And Mrs. Pleasanton means to go to her native district, as soon as her daughter is provided for also."

"You are a happy woman not to have a marrying mamma. What persecution you escape, great heiress though you are."

"That's right, throw my gold into my face But, truly, I am getting old. London life is killing.

Would you come to the church when I become a nun?"

"I am a scientific man who rarely goes to church. When I do, please God,—there's a contradictory prayer for you !—it will be for a happier occasion than to see you put on a black veil."

"You mean a marriage! Carroll, don't start like that, or all eyes will be upon us; that's the nearest you ever came yet to a proposal. But —now do not speak and break the charm of such an avowal—I shall not be so rich—it is Naomi is the favourite child! I—"

"In good heaven's name what have I done to be so mistaken?" cried Rendall. "Our position relatively, my—besides, to remove all possibility of misconception, let me tell you that my heart is another's."

She pointed over the sea to some beams of light from the lighthouse, merely to prevent the bystanders suspecting their colloquy had been so intimate.

"Yes, as well expect those headlands to come together!" said Rendall, bitterly.

"But this tunnel will link them."

"By underhand means, Miss Millward!" returned Rendall, fiercely, at the way the coquette clung to her prey in spite of a rebuff which ought to have vanquished any other woman but that hild of Mammon. "Above-board, let this end all : I love another!"

Twenty minutes afterwards, Miss Millward was chatting with Henry Pleasanton as amiably as became a sister-in-law *in futuro*.

Suddenly she directed his eyes to Rendall, whom Goddard was boring to extract a remedy gratis for a cold in the head with which that victim to the rushing ozone was suffering.

" Henry," she said, " as heaven shines on us, I will forgive you all the past, and you shall live peacefully with Naomi. Only kill that man for me. He has mortally insulted me."

By the glitter in her eyes, by her accent, her anditor divined what mine he had been foolishly walking beside.

" I kill a man ! preposterous ! " he faltered.

" But we are approaching a land where it may be done. A chemist, a man who bows his back over orris-root and plumbago, a student who does not know a pistol from a popgun ! Surely you could slay him offhand."

" Thank you. I don't mind telling you," as his mouth burned again, " I could have had a duel in London."

" Henry, kill him, and I'll wed —— in order that you may within twenty years be chief of the State."

" Calais, gentlemen ! " said the captain of the yacht. " Pleasant run across, Miss Millward."

" I never enjoyed myself more," replied the heiress, graciously. " Let the steward give each

man a five-pound note to enjoy themselves in port.
We may be here a week."

"A week, miss?   Time enough for a sailor to
wed, fight, and be buried!"

CHAPTER XXV

MAKING up his mind to return to England in some vessel not sailing under the colours copied from Miss Millward's favourite lapis-lazuli and gold splashes, Carroll rose in the morning to hurry over breakfast and run to the *poste restante* for the letter Marcia had promised him to be on the way at the same time as he. He was surprised to see the man hand him out a large packet as well as the note, both addressed in her hand. A profound terror seized him.

"That infernal woman is bad luck," said he. "Marcia has been hurt at the attentions I paid her in common courtesy, and she has returned all my little presents during our too brief acquaintance. The successor of Blandford has been successful!"

His apprehension prevented him opening even the letter there. He went back to the hotel. The letter was worded in the following terms :—

"DEAR MR. RENDALL,—All is well here. Naomi came over, but I have been dreadfully lonely without you. That is all the home intelligence. The enormous bale of goods which should be received with this, unless the train and steamer break down under the mass, and which has nearly ruined me in postage stamps—I had to buy out Gratchley P.O.—was given me by poor Fordice. He met with some accident in town, about which he is very reticent to me, and his leg is nearly as bad as when first broken, the doctor says. He says the papers belong to you, and that you will understand how to act when you look at them. I promised him, in your name, that you would ' do all that became a man ' to oblige a fellow-worker, and that seemed to soothe him.

"Yours sincerely, MARCIA PLEASANTON."

Only then he noticed on the envelope flap some almost effaced pencil marks : Marcia had hastily added, after closing :

" F is dead. Do oblige him."

He sat down relieved of his chief terror.

" Of course," he said, as he unbound the formidable packet, " I shall be the poor fellow's executor. I might have been injured in twenty ways by those stupid craftsmen if he had not warned me, and even struck in for me. Rough, uncouth, there was true steel—polished steel under the red shirt."

The papers spread out, the parchments unrolled partly as they had been on the table of Mr. Chafferwell, half an hour later Carroll Rendall went down on his knees and prayed for the repose of the soul of the father whom he had never known, whom he had seen only to regard as of coarser clay. Then he bound up the papers, to be placed in the hotel safe, with a letter to be forwarded to England if he did not call for them next day. He went to a tailor's and obtained a black suit, with a frock coat made for a military man, and otherwise appeared in mourning, strict, severe gloomy—a Manfred in modern apparel—at the Casino.

The season was over : the Casino was let for the banquet and ball to follow. It was illuminated with electric lights. There was no difficulty therefore in Rendall singling out the man he sought, resisting on the way through the crowd the invitations to drink in the English mode, with scientific worthies from Paris and Germany and Italy, proud to have known the young rising luminary by correspondence.

At the moment he drew nigh to Mr. Henry Pleasanton that captivating gentleman was completing the charm over an old gentleman in blue glasses and his three daughters, by promising them a month's entertainment at his Lincolnshire estate, when they came to summer in Albion.

" My name is Wightwarden, as you see by my card—"

He had uttered so much when the shadow of the tall figure of the young professor fell upon him, and, speaking slowly in French, so that the whole assembly almost could distinguish every syllable in the lull in the music, Rendall was heard to interrupt :

"You are a liar, Henry Pleasanton. I am the last of the Lincolnshire Wightwardens; as witness my hand, where my father's left its unresented stigma !"

With which he gave Mr. Henry Pleasanton a backhander across the mouth, which deposited him in the arms of Mr. Blandford just so as to prevent the blood from his cut lip besprinkling Miss Millward's ball dress. Removing his glove and trampling on it as if it had been disgraced, the author of a rare scene of confusion left the group and the Casino. He walked about till morning, but even then had not tired the tiger in his bosom. As soon as he could do so, he entered the hotel and wrote a letter to Marcia. It was more curt than her own.

"DEAR MISS PLEASANTON,—Whatever is the outcome of this day's hostile encounter between your brother and your sincere friend, we can never meet again. Therefore I can say that I love you, and shall die loving you, none other ever.

"Yours, with respect and sorrow,
       "RAYMOND WIGHTWARDEN,
"whom you have known as *Carroll Rendall*."

In the meantime Henry Pleasanton had been removed to his hotel. The lip being cut, his mouth was not swollen. Blandford and Goddard were with him, having promised to see him through the affair, for now he was determined to fight.

"It is I who have the choice," he mused. "A chance in my favour, by which I shall profit. Cicely shall be content with me."

"Will he come up to the scratch?" queried Goddard, recalling the scene with old Wight-warden.

"I think so. Nothing is more dangerous than a coward in a white heat," returned Blandford. "Henry," he proceeded, going into the room where Pleasanton was writing home, "they are all for swords here." He took up a cane. "I can give you a wrinkle. Mark me—you come on guard at a distance, engaging very little of your blade. He is a hot-headed fellow, this pestle-pounder, he will run at you. You yield, with sweeping *parade*, and when you find yourself pressed, as he makes a lunge, you beat his blade to your right, turning the point of your right foot; and as he passes spit him like a frog, in the side or back. They may call it murder! but he will die all the same."

"No," said Henry, lifting his head from the basin, where he was sponging the lower part of his face in cold water to keep down the in-flammation, "I am not acquainted with the sword."

"But, my dear fellow, this wizard assisted Krupp in perfecting his rampart-repeater ; *ergo,* he is experienced in fire-arms. Goddard, do you know if he shoots ? "

" No."

"My dear chappie, I must kill the brute. I see, from the acquaintances I made last night, that there is money to be made, position to be attained in France simultaneously with my progress at home. No legal decision in England now will permit my reception here unless I go out with the brute, and slay him ; and I can only do that my own way. We are both novices with the sword, and novices always wound one another—hardly ever kill. It is not necessary I should have published it, but I have cultivated pistol practice. I tried to choose my accomplishments judiciously, and I have a notion of hitting him there." He touched Blandford a little above the hip. "There, you see ? because a little higher is risky, the arm comes in your way ; whereas here, you tear into a number of fine, delicate, and vital organs. Let it be arranged in what they term the American style here, I think, firing at will. And now go to him and arrange matters. I must finish writing home to tranquillise them there. I shall not stir out just yet. I must bathe my face to calm down and be more presentable. I am not very much marked, am I ? I shall have my dinner brought to me here.

When you return we might find a shooting gallery. Arrange as if for yourself, and thanks beforehand."

After Blandford had called on Rendall (as we continue to entitle him) the latter saw that he had no friends there, consequently no seconds. Until then he had not thought of this. He took a stroll, but there was no acquaintance to be encountered of the kind he sought. He returned empty-handed to his hotel. He had never felt more lonely. He turned into the café which formed the ground-floor.

Swords and military caps were hanging against the wall. At the further end of the room, through clouds of tobacco-smoke, uniforms were seen moving round the threadbare cloth of a billiard table. A little sickly waiter with a white apron was skimming about, scared and terrified, pouring the coffee on the *Moniteur de l'Armée* instead of into the cups.

Near the counter, a drum-major, reinstated in taller feather after the annulled abolition of the drums, was playing backgammon with the master of the café, who was in his shirt-sleeves. On all sides voices were calling to one another, and replying in the rough tones of soldiers fresh from the autumn manœuvres.

"To-morrow I'm going to see the Troupe Pomponnet, with one veritable Parisian star—I shall spend my eight days in town—Harresas is now a sacristan at St. Sulpice's : he has passed the inspection—Who is on duty at the Fisherman's Ball Saloon ?—What an idea to lampoon the colonel's niece when you have no marks against you in your book."

These were all infantry soldiers from the fort waiting tattoo at nine o'clock.

"Waiter, a bowl of punch and *three* glasses," cried Rendall, sitting down at a table where were two of the blue coats with red epaulettes, with which his funereal costume contrasted.

When the punch was brought he filled the three glasses, pushed one to each soldier, and rising, glass in hand, with a bow which the shade of Beau Brummell might have fashioned, said politely :

" I beg to drink your health, gentlemen. You are military men, I the grandson of a soldier who fought against your forefathers at Waterloo, but son of a soldier who fought beside you in Italy. I have a duel on, and am alone here. I am sure, however, that I need go no farther to fare worse."

" You don't look like a soldier," began one, drinking none the less and eying him critically.

" But you don't look like a poltroon," went on the other. " I shall be glad of a diversion,"

" And I always keep step with Gailarbin," said the second soldier.

They finished the punch. Rendall had fallen in with the descendants of the men-at-arms in

·'Généviève de Brabant." They marched to the conference with Blandford, and the meeting was fixed for four o'clock, on the beach near Ouessant, weapons, pistols ; method, to fire at will after the regulation word of command.

Blandford sent on Goddard ahead, and found them both in a shooting gallery, Henry amusing himself in firing at bundles of four or five matches hanging by a string, which he lighted with bullets grazing their tips.

" But that is child's play," he remarked to his friends. " I believe that they take fire with the wind of the ball; but see what I have done certainly with the pills."

He showed them a target, in the inner circle of which he had made a dozen " centres."

" This afternoon at four o'clock, as you wished," said Blandford.

" He has officers for his seconds," continued Goddard, who felt that he would be a hero at the club. " A *chasseur* and a *pandour*," airing his French.

·'Good," said Henry, handing his pistol to the attendent. " All goes satisfactorily."

Lest the people at the hotel should make some objection, for all the town were cognisant of the *fracas* in the Casino, the predominant opinion being that Mr. Chamberlain and Sir Edward had pelted one another at the buffet with cheesecakes, the two breakfasted at Blandford's lodgings—the

prudent fox kept an apartment in Calais all
the year round.

Henry was gay, unreserved, and talked freely.
When the surgeon arrived the four entered the
carriage in waiting.

Halfway—they had all been silent until then
—Henry impatiently threw his cigar out of the
window.

" Give me a smoke, Blandford, a good one. You
don't know how important a good cigar is for
shooting. To shoot well, you must not be nervous.
That's the first condition. I took care to have a
shower-bath this morning. If you have the least
tremor—now driving, for instance, is fatal. The
horses pull at your hand. I defy you after that
exercise to take a true aim; you have always a
jerking in your finger. Those old novels are absurd,
with their duels where the dead-shot arrives on
the ground throwing the reins to his servant ! "

Goddard, with the air of a connoisseur, approved
the observations with a nod. He was thinking
that, as M. Gailarbin was a "midget " beside him,
and seconds sometimes made it a round game,
perhaps, he could be a hero of the duello himself.
Blandford said nothing; he was afraid that
Pleasanton talked too much, if not a braggart.

When they arrived, Rendall and his seconds
were waiting on the road between the sea and the
sand-mounds. The united parties proceeded in-
land a little.

The ground was white with salt, which had been drying up all the morning. The bare branches of the trees rose in the sky, and in the distance a few twigs showed perfectly black against the red glow of the wintry sunset.

The paces were counted, the pistols loaded, and the combatants placed in position. Two canes laid on the blanched sands marked the limit of the ten paces, within which each must remain.

At the moment when Blandford led Pleasanton to the place which a draw of long or short straws had allotted to him, and as he was hiding a corner of his shirt-collar which appeared outside his necktie, his man said, "Thanks," in a low voice; "my heart beats a little, old fellow! but I shall satisfy your ideal."

Rendall removed his frock-coat, tore off his scarf, and threw it away from him. His shirt, open in front, showed his broad and powerful chest, and he looked, to the admiration of his seconds, less of a professor and more like a soldier than they had thought possible.

The combatants being armed, the seconds all withdrew to the same side, and Blandford, having the word to give, said clearly :

" Fire !—One—two—three ! "

At the last word, Carroll, firing, continued to advance, walking without attempts to guard himself with arms or smoking pistol. Pleasanton had stopped, rocked as if hit, but it was fear ; then the blood flowing again from his heart, and his joy kindling with his bounding gratification and thirst for vengeance on the man who had given him such a mortal fright, he took up the march. But his antagonist had already crossed the imaginary line which marked the half-way between their original stands. It looked as if he meant to tread down the other, as a dragoon rushes at a foot soldier.

At length, the time seeming long to the bystanders, they met. Or to be more exact, Henry Pleasanton's extended pistol touched the breast of his adversary. The latter stopped short, like a tug-boat of which the hawser had not been cast off by forgetfulness, brought up all standing by the tightening of the tether. Henry thrust out the long barrel a little more, as if to test the firmness of the obstacle; but Carroll stood unflinching, though he felt his flesh well up into the muzzle, whilst the ice-cold ring dented a circle.

The agony of awaiting was so intense upon Goddard that he almost shrieked: "Do fire!" but Blandford pointed to the French soldiers, who bore themselves stiffly, as much as to say, "Let them not despise us English!"

Meanwhile, Henry had stared into the other's eyes with all his venomous hate, and thereupon feeling that the situation was wavering on the narrow space between the sublime and the ridiculous, he decided for the tragic, and pulled the trigger. There was a report, muffled like that when boys thrust the muzzle of a toy cannon into a bottle; and whilst Rendall swung round and clapped his hand to his heart, the smoke seemed to follow a flow of sparks up into Pleasanton's face; the latter sent out a scream, and flinging the pistol afar with a convulsive throwing up of both hands, he fell to the ground as if he had been broken at the wheel, in a heap, all his muscles at the joints relaxing.

The pressure of the pistol mouth had choked it up and rendered the long barrel air-tight. The bullet had been unable to overcome the resistance of the compressed column of air, had recoiled on the expanding gas from the powder, and, a flaw in the touch-hole lending its aid to the catastrophe, Henry's pistol had been shattered, and the nipple and a fragment attached had torn through his throat into his brain.

"By Jove!" cried Goddard, while the dead man was looked to by the surgeon, who significantly closed his instrument case, and Blandford curiously went to pick up the damaged firearm. "You have good nerves, Mr. Rendall; you're a wonder."

"I am not hurt," said the professor to the surgeon. "Mr. Goddard, my name from this moment is Raymond Wightwarden, and I do not think any one will dispute it again."

He turned on his heel, donned his coat and

returned to town with his seconds.   On the way
he looked up at the sky where coldly gleamed the
star Marcia had once, he remembered, called hers.
and sighed :

"Poor girl ! "

CHAPTER XXVI.

MARCIA, unable to resist the loneliness she had mentioned, and strangely picturing in her mind all that might be supposed to appear of the communing of the professor and Miss Millward on the steam yacht, had gone over to the Hall to stay the night with Naomi, all alone.

The colonel, puzzled at hearing nothing from his son, went to the station at noon. There alighted out of the train, presently in, two passengers: Mr. Goddard and the confidential agent. The latter bowed ceremoniously to the veteran and went forward to look after the luggage.

"I cannot say I expected to see you," exclaimed the colonel, astonished. "Is Henry—"

"Dear colonel," began Goddard, as he pressed his hands.

"Well? what's the matter?" said Colonel Pleasanton, who felt the hand quiver. "Henry—"

"Well, he's wounded."

"An accident coming over? I had Millward's telegram; you crossed in lovely weather."

"A pistol flew to pieces in his hand," went

on Goddard, breathing more freely as he saw Blandford coming up to his relief.

"Oh, an accident?—wounded?—dangerously? What the devil had he to do with firearms?"

"It was a duel," said Blandford, forming a kind of screen with his friend before an oblong box on a truck between two porters.

"A duel! oh, on French ground! true. Has he fought?"

Goddard hung his head, and the agent nodded.

"Wounded, you say? Oh, no! he is *dead!*" for he saw the case of ominous shape.

"Dead!" mechanically repeated the old soldier. His hands opened as if they let a broken sword fall. Tears coming with the words, he added, "But his poor mother! Lotte! Henry gone. Great God! You don't know how she loves him! Only thirty—a boy!"

Choking with sobs, he fell on the seat against the wall. "Is that he?" faltered the Colonel, pointing to the dread box.

It was taken up to the house, and the body placed on the bed in Henry's room,

"Thank you!" said the father, shaking his head to intimate that he was unable to say more.

In his oblivion he mechanically shook hands with the porters, instead of giving them money, as if they, too, were gentlemen and his friends.

"Who will break the news to his sister?" inquired Goddard, in an undertone.

"Not I, no more than to his mother," rejoined Blandford.

Colonel Pleasanton had heard them. He wheeled round from gazing on the dead face, blackening, though drained by the wound, where the many stitches in silver wire gleamed, and said :

"Nor I, gentlemen. Come down into the grounds, please; we must cast lots for that." He strode forth, let them pass him, locked the door, and led the way into the garden.

Then, in silence, the three went four or five times round the central parterre. Tears filled the colonel's eyes, but he no longer wept. Now and then, words seemed to hover on his lips, and then to sink back into his heart. At length, in a low and quivering voice, looking at Blandford, whom he abruptly fixed with his eyes, he said, in a tone of command, as to a soldier :

"Take the best horse, and Marcia's, ride over to Beechbrake, and bring her back. It is she who is the proper person to inform her mother that we have no son."

With the feeling that he was well out of the painful quandary, Blandford obeyed, murmuring :

"Cicely will have already let her into the tale. I shall meet her half-way, in tears, and much may be done with a weeping woman when a man has an oily tongue."

When he had gone, the colonel turned upon Mr. Goddard, and curtly demanded :

"Did he die bravely?"

The swarthy young gentleman turned pale, and stammered an account of the duel, but, garble it as he would, it was evident that after the professor had fired, all the honours were to him as the brave man.

"Thank you," said Colonel Pleasanton, frowning, his tears disappearing like the last moisture when the simoom speeds along. "You have done your duty gallantly."

"By Jove!" ejaculated Goddard, as he followed the colonel, "I thought he would fly off and pop at Rendall straight: He has not even asked who it was met him. The fact is, Henry was not the sort of fellow one would want to avenge!"

Which was the epitaph of the cold yet brilliant young man.

There is no doubt Miss Millward expected a courier from Gratchtey, for she was up at a window, and had Mr. Blandford brought directly into her presence.

"She's not gone," thought he. "She has not told the girls. I suppose she kept her father in town also to prevent their knowing it."

"You and your accomplice are a praiseworthy pair," cried Miss Millward. "You have perpetrated a downright murder!"

"What do you mean? The biter was bit, that's all. Henry was a rank assassin, and his weapon turned on him."

"You should have arranged the affair when you saw that Rendall meant a fight."

"He did not mean to fight him. He missed him deliberately—his bullet cut a tree ten feet overhead. Arrange an affair like that, after a blow—after two, I should say, if Goddard doesn't lie when he says the insult was 'twice-laid,' as your yacht commander words it."

"You had better tell his father that."

"You'll catch me. He is a soldier. But you had better tell him you sent his boy to the death."

"Stop! Do not interfere with me, Blandford."

"At the risk of having a bravo let loose at me with a pistol that will stand a bursting-charge? Profit by the disaster, my queen! Give out that Henry shot himself because his love for you was hopeless, and he saw no escape but to die. But we forget that poor father mourning over his son. It is astonishing how precious a scamp is when he can wreak no more mischief. Where is Miss Pleasanton to know of this? Here, or in the room with the corpse?"

"You heartless wretch! I will tell her."

"She will shriek the house down."

"Marcia? You do not know her! You do not, or she would not have refused you. I will tell her to bear up, so as to repeat the sad tidings to Naomi."

"Good idea! You are clever. I will await you. Let me cast up accounts," continued Mr.

Blandford when Cicely had left him. " Henry owes
twenty pounds—the father is good for that. If
the mother loves her husband, I can squeeze her
for another five hundred, for to know the family
secret will just about finish the old warrior. Or
it will be a pressure upon Miss Marcia. She let
me down easy, but it was a *quietus*. We must
toss : money or charming young lady. Lady !
Here she is ! "

Cicely brought Marcia into the room. She
gave Mr. Blandford one sharp look; but he was
master of his countenance ; she could not say he
was glad to be the messenger that caused her
pain.

" You understand," said Miss Millward, taking
the girl's hand, awed and perplexed by seeing her
so calm after the first shock, " your brother has
been killed in a duel ! "

Miss Pleasanton said nothing.

" His enemy ought not to have known anything
of the assumption of his name. He never read
the paper. He never saw any body on the
subject ! "

Blandford dared not smile.

" Who do you mean ? " inquired Marcia, thinking of something else.

" Wightwarden," said Blandford.

" And his son—"

" You have not named the antagonist."

" Oh, I beg your pardon; Raymond Wightwarden

with whom he fought, is the son of the man on your
father's pay list, the workman whom you knew as
Fordice—"

" Fordice ? " reiterated the girl, not yet enlight-
•ned, and involuntarily glancing at Blandford, who
doubted now that she had witnessed his going to
Fordice's cottage.

" Some one told him of the name being taken ;
some one brought him and his son together after
twenty—twenty-five years ! "

" But this son — this son ? " queried Marcia
feverishly.

"Carroll Rendall ! " hissed Cicely, unable to
speak calmly any longer, when the revelation of
Marcia's heart was to follow in the next minute.

" Carroll ! " ejaculated Marcia. " Carroll his
son ! Oh, those papers ! I am the enemy of my
brother, who brought father and son in contact.
It was I who carried out Fordice's last wishes by
sending his papers to Carroll. It is I who have
killed my brother !"

Marcia had stood erect, her eyes starting with
horror. She moved her lips, her mouth opened, she
tried to repeat " It was I ! " Suddenly carrying
her hand to her heart, she fell into Cicely's arms.

" You're beaten all round the compass," sneered
Blandford. "You proud devil ! she loves him, d'ye
see ? "

" What do I care who loves him ? The question
is, does he love another than me ? "

"It is my business to answer questions," returned the agent. He held up the letter which Carroll had posted to Marcia, which the butler had given him to carry to her, and which he had read on the journey with as little hesitation as a clerk in the Dead Letter Office. "There—'I love you—none other ever!'"

With an exclamation which horrified Blandford, Cicely lifted up the insensible form in her embrace as if to dash it down on the floor, but the agent sprang forward and took her by the throat with a grasp so rough that if she had been wearing a necklace, the jewel points must have injured her.

"By heaven! if you ever harm her while I live, I'll lodge you in Newgate!" he cried, reckless who heard him.

Then he snatched Marcia from her embrace, whilst the tall blonde reeled back and back till the table under the broad pier-glass checked her retreat. He marched out of the room, afraid to look behind, spite of his violence, and heartily pleased when he had reached the horses without being in any way detained. The servants were preparing a carriage, at Naomi's suggestion, but he rejected anything from that house, and holding Marcia up in the saddle, the two horses bounded off side by side.

"From this moment forward," said the horseman, gloomily, "you are condemned, Owen Blandford, to eggs, lemons, and wine out of your own bottles. For I am much mistaken if Miss Millward does not essay on your vile carcass some of that poison with which she attempted her father's life, and against the repetition of which patricide he has cleverly prepared a will by which his death will not liberally benefit her."

Behind him he had, indeed, revived that beauty's heart-hunger for revenge. She looked at her throat, where lurid marks were darkening, as on the face of that man whom she had undeniably driven to death, and hoarsely said :—

" Carroll loves that girl—yes, yes ; but this villain loves her too ! If I can but make them meet ! they are men who will kill one another."

CHAPTER XXVII.

PLAINLY to speak, the grief of the Pleasantons at the loss of the heir who promised to attain such an altitude was tempered. Mr. Perch thought it very remarkable; and would say, " That family reminds me of one long troubled with a black sheep which consoles itself, when at last he has been locked up, that they will be anxious about him no more."

The colonel, in a species of wonder that a son of his could be a coward, wondered still more profoundly at the unexpected mood of his wife. He had expected the shock to kill her outright. On the contrary, it seemed to lighten her of a burden. But suddenly after that temporary recovery, she sank into gloomy apathy. She continued indifferent, silent, abstracted, She spent her days and nights in attendance upon her pining daughter, uncomplaining, patient, always the same docile, humble Dorcas; but all was performed, as it were, mechanically. The spirit had departed from her caresses; her attentions were such as emanate sheerly from an automatic sense of duty.

Marcia was in a decline; doubly she was doomed. Even if Carroll loved her, as she thought, for Blandford had taken care to say nothing of the suppressed letter from the professor which would have cleared up that question, she could not hope to have her love blessed for the man who had faced her brother in mortal combat, and whom she had set upon the vanquished one, unwittingly, but as fatally as when one touches that spring which kills his mandarin. Mr. Blandford had been to see her several times, but only by chance caught a glimpse of her.

"Fallen off lamentably," he said to himself. " I must prosecute that affair which concerns her mother. That may be the elixir by which those rare charms will be restored."

The faculty, represented by famous representatives, for Millward, urged by Naomi, exerted his influences, could make nothing of Marcia's despair. Sisters never grieved so excessively for their brothers in any of the books.

Now began for the old soldier the sorrowful existence of those from whom hope has fled, and who look for a life of anguish and dread, full of trepidation honourably borne. He was the outpost rashly advanced too far from support, who knew beyond doubting that the enemy would cut him off before relief could possibly come up at his alarum shot.

Like those about the invalid, he indulged in

bitterness, while he reproached himself for his weakness. He tormented himself with accusations, saying that he was to blame for not having done all that ought to have been done ; that Marcia might perhaps have been saved, if he had sooner consulted the medical men ; if at such a time, in such a month, on such and such a day, he had thought of something vitally material.

With Marcia's wasting away, he was consumed by the fever of his grief. Solitude, darkness, and silence brought no relief. One image, thin, faded, ghostly, flickered before him. His daughter, always his dear daughter! His imagination was disturbed by his anxiety ; his fears became insupportable. At last, the foe, Marcia's eternal enemy, Death, had daunted the man who had so long derided him. In the morning, he would partially wake up, when, like a man half asleep who instinctively turns away from the light, he would again court sleep, endeavouring to escape if but for a few short moments from the painful consciousness of sorrow.

With the day returned old torments, and the father was compelled to restrain himself, to be cheerful, to respond to those smiles of patient suffering, to mournful echoes of the madcap's ringing jests, to those decaying illusions which build on the shifting sands of the future, to those heart-rending words of hopefulness with which the dying delude themselves.

In the weak, tender failing tones of an invalid, Marcia would say : "How pleasant it is to give good-bye at last to pain! Oh, how I shall enjoy existence, when I am quite well again."

And her father would answer : " Yes, of course you will, that's the recompense of a just heaven !" But each word was accented with a tear.

It was not until the colonel was forced to go over Henry's papers as an executor, that he discovered that his workman Fordice was his old companion-in-arms, and the first challenger of his son ; and that the heir to the usurped name was his experimental chemist, Carroll. He said not a word to Marcia : he understood all. She had already learnt it, or, with the prescience of one near the grave, divined the enigma.

The ailing have faith in the curative powers of places where they were wont to be happy. Certain spots recur to them with the smile of a native land, and the sweetness of cradle songs. As an infant totters towards its nurse's arms, their hopes turn for refuge to some country house, some sea-side cabin, some home in the glen where they were born, and whence death seems banished.

Marcia began to think of Elmwood, of which her mother had dropped many a hint, as if she wished to fly from a nearness to London. The girl flattered herself that once there, she would be out of pain. She felt sure of that. The fumes of the Works were making her ill. She had been most happy at Elmwood. And with the desire of change and necessity for motion, which restlessness fosters, this idea took firm hold of her imagination. She spoke of it to her father and dinned him with it. It would interfere with nothing. The manager, was a trustworthy man. They could return in the autumn.

"When do we start, papa dear?" she repeated every day with more impatience. "Naomi is going to winter in Madeira, and soon leaves for Naples, to acclimatise her to the true sunlight. Mamma wishes to see Elmwood too. Let us go."

It was the "Let us go thither" of Mignon, an irresistible prayer.

In fact, Naomi's visits were injurious; the two girls thought of Henry, if they never breathed his name, and Marcia revolted at the constant curb which prevented her stripping the young girl's idol of its gilding and paint.

Of course the colonel yielded. His daughter promised him so persistently a benefit from the journey, that at last he began to believe it himself. In this longing, he almost saw that lucky inspiration from relenting Fate, which the invalid feels at the turn to convalescence.

The doctor said, "Yes, perhaps North-country air is the thing!" like a man accustomed to those fancies of the dying, who think to cheat Death by moving out of his path.

The family departed for Elmwood.

The pleasure and excitement of the journey, the nervous vigour which it imparts to the weakest, the breeze through the open carriage window, sustained the invalid as far as Wetterburn. They gave Marcia one day to rest there, and the next morning installed her in the best carriage that could procured, and left for Elmwood. The road was villanous, the journey long and irksome. Mrs. Pleasanton dozed on the front seat. The colonel supported his daughter, with his arm under the pillow on which she leant, reminded of a similar experience in an improvised ambulance upon the Cordilleras. That time he had a corpse in his arms, when, having fallen asleep, he woke up with an arm almost as dead. He shuddered at the omen. But the jolting benefited her in the same way as old men are galvanized by the shaking of an omnibus. She roused up notably as they neared "home," and quite audibly exclaimed :

"Oh, look, papa! There's the great poplar standing; no, it's broken! The little boys used to fish for leeches in that pond. I can hear their wails of mingled joy and pain when the nasty beasts fastened on their toes!"

At a little wood near the village her father had to get out and pick the floweret from the edge of the ditch which she pointed out to him.

"Rosy, papa! the colour of dawn!" she said, kissing it.

Their by-road took them past the Brumsey Inn, the first straggling houses, the general-dealer's, the farrier's, the young walnut tree, the church, the watchmaker's; the labourers were a-field. Children who were playing, yelped "School Board! Bogey!" and scampered away. An old man in an embroidered smock-frock, seated on a bench before his door, shivering in the sun, took off his cap.

Soon the horses stopped. The carriage-door was opened, and a man, waiting before a vine-clad porch, took Miss Pleasanton in his arms, and carried her in.

"Dear-a me!" he said, as he "hefted" before he actually lifted her; "our poor young lady weighs no more than a sack o' flowwer."

"I hope you are hale, Keywright," said the colonel heartily, lightly slapping the shoulder of the old gardener who had been formerly in his service.

The next and following days Marcia experienced delightful moments of reverie, in which the morning over heaven and earth mingled with the renewal of thoughts, known to the morning of her life.

Supported, almost carried, by her father, she wished to see everything,—the garden, the fruit trees, the grass plot before the house, the shady burns, the pond, with its green mantle of stagnant water, striped with dull yellow. Her feet traced the old pathways. The ruins appeared to have grown much older. She found the furrow where she had buried a little dog among ancient warriors, so the parish clerk had said.

"He was white, papa, my dear little ' Lily.' "

"And you would not let the lily remain unpainted. Your mother wrote me that you wanted to dye him red and blue, in honour of the anniversary of some battle you thought I had figured in."

They laughed together.

There was no doubt that she brightened up. Her strength returned, she talked boldly of dispensing with her father's arm. And one day she forbade him even to follow her, and took only Keywright to carry a basket for ferns.

"It is too dry that way, miss," said the old servant. " No ferns ever seen at Wightwarden."

Wightwarden !

"Keywright, what does that name mean?" she asked hastily, as if to cover her confusion.

"Doan't'ee know, miss? It's schoolmaster's work to answer that. 'Wight' means strong; and ' warden ' is a guardsman. Them Wightwardens kept the borders ever so long ago, and they were swashing fighting men. Nothing that carried a sword could daunt 'em. The Fairfields is nothing to them—they come over fro' France a lang time after. The Wightwardens were proud—prouder than the Fairfields! The last of them that I knowed—you'd not a catched him a-marrying his housemaid, 'cause she was beauteous,—race for ever ! He were a soldier, ay, a grand old fighting companys."

This speaker had known the father of Carroll then !

"Are you tired?" said she, with affectionate interest in the aged soldier. " I am not; but, if you like, we will rest, or turn back. But I should like to see those ruins of the castle."

" It's Fort Alice, miss, so we call it. You forgot that! She's forgotten that," he chuckled.

" The Fortalice ! yes. Show me the way."

The half-dozen lumps of stone which still projected above the weeds on a mound, were a paltry foundation for musings upon chivalry. Nevertheless, a gentleman in a tourist suit was to be seen standing among them, moving his hand in what seemed conjuring. But a few steps after, Marcia saw that he was directing the advance from the opposite side of three or four men with a muffled bundle upon a hand-barrow.

" You must come another time, miss. It's one of them ' 'Merricans on tower,' with his ' How do you do, squire ?' and 'What's the average wages of your farm hands in these parts ? ' "

" Oh ! " she whispered, turning pale and retreating to rest on his arm.

In setting down their load the men had clumsily displaced its covering, and by the shape of the box, Marcia judged that it enveloped a coffin. She looked at the gentleman in tweed, and was angry at his not being known to her. It was the feeling when a play, for which your imagination has anticipated one ending, takes a fresh turn and concludes with an unexpected climax. But while she trembled on her escort's arm, a gentleman in black came up the slope, his profile turned to her, and she murmured:

"Carroll!"

It was Carroll. At last Mr. Chafferwell had triumphed over all quirks and trammels, and the last of the Wightwardens had brought his father's remains to rest in the ground which the first had wrested from the Saxons.

CHAPTER XXVIII.

THE relapse in which the alarmed Keywright brought his young mistress home was serious, and all the more distressful to the colonel from the recent improvement. She had besought the old servant to keep quiet about the view of the preparations for burial, which was all that had given her a shock. But Pleasanton made inquiries : he heard of the consecration of the grave, and knew what vision from the past had wrecked his darling's health again. He marvelled again that no chord within him was stirred by the impudence of his son's slayer appearing as a neighbour to the bereaved parents. He questioned Marcia vaguely.

"Love!" she repeated at an inquiry more than usually distinct. "I could never love any one. You made me too hard to please. I was perfectly sure beforehand that no one would love me like you. I saw so many expressions pass over your face, when I was by, fraught with joy ; and when we went anywhere together, were you not proud of me? Father, it was vain for any one to love

me. I should never have found another to spoil
me in your way."

"Very fine; but this reasoning will not prevent
my good little girl falling in love with some handsome young man one of these days, when she is
herself again."

"Oh! your handsome young man is very far
off," said Marcia, with a dubious smile in her
eyes. "It appears singular that I have no more
a desire to marry than to be a nun. It's all your
fault. But I do not repine. I had everything at
home, and never imagined any other happiness.
Why should I change? I was quite happy!
Life was so sweet among you all and my heart
so contented! Yet perhaps," said she, after a
moment's silence, "if I had been like some unfortunate girls, badgered, cooped up, constrained,
misunderstood, with no such father as you, I
would have escaped like others, in my wish to be
loved. I should have thought of marriage as a
romantic kind of escape from prison. Still I should
have always found it difficult to fall in love. The
idea never seemed to convene with my tastes; it has
always set me laughing, as at a bad joke. You
must remember, about the time of my sister's marriage, while Pryse-Price was a daily visitor?
Didn't I tease them rarely? My castles in the
air were mostly untenanted. I could look through
the long corridors and spy no long-plumed prince;
go to the windows and see no knight on the green

sward, with his lancepennon of scarlet serpentining across the blue sky. How strange, when you come to think of it. Papa, is the sky blue everywhere?" raising herself in her invalid's chair.

"All round the world so? Yes. I wish it were more blue here, though, to-day. There are some clouds gathering; I feel a storm in my wounds."

"Oh, I am a barometer, too, papa! I could have told you that. When you are ill, the sky seems nearer you than before."

"You have been tiring yourself reading, my darling. Let us go on talking instead. What is the old thing you have found in the dusty bookcase?" He stretched his hand towards the book, which slipped from her thin fingers into his. On opening it, he noticed some pages which he had turned down many years, in order that the little lass might not read them. The forbidden pages were still turned down, though the grown woman would not have seen a word to shun in them.

Marcia appeared to slumber. The stormy precursor did affect her. An insupportable heaviness oppressed her, and at the same time she was filled with nervous uneasiness. Electricity pervaded the air. A deep silence spread, and the sudden hushing, as it passed across the country, had caused her a sensation of intense anxiety. She looked at the time-piece, and twitched her hands.

"Ah! yes, it's true," said the colonel. "There's a black cloud, a great cloud over the Fortalice.

Here it comes! and it thickens. We shall have it heavy! Shall I close the window and draw the blind, and have the lamp lighted?"

"No," said Marcia, quickly; "no light in the day-time. No, no. I am not afraid of anything that comes from above. I wish you would go and see if mamma is prepared; you know she cannot bear lightning."

"Nay, it is still far off," said the colonel, lingering.

"Hark! there's the rain," cried Marcia, in a tone of relief. "Rain is like dew—good enough to drink! Oh, here is mamma!"

Mrs. Pleasanton came in hurriedly, a shawl over her head, as if she had sought to seal her ears up against the thunderpeals. She was yellow as an old nun; her mouth had fallen in, for in her apprehension, she had forgotten to replace her false teeth. She trembled to an excess. Nevertheless, she waved her husband away, as much as to say that she only sought company; and, lying down on the sofa in the darkest corner, she muffled up her head, and they only knew of her existence by her moans after each thunder-clap.

Large drops began to fall slowly, then faster, then the rain descended in torrents. The storm enveloped Elmwood. The thunder rolled and crashed, for an instant the country was in a blaze, the next in the deepest shadow, out of which from the wood before the ruins of the Wightwarden's stronghold, the colonel fancied he saw stalk forth towards his house the grim, crippled workman, as Goddard described him, to lash his son.

The two women, young and old, quivered and breathed hard. The old soldier sat up stiffly, grasping a chair before him.

All at once, the two women opened their eyes, and Mrs. Pleasanton turned round to face the window. There seemed to be a scream in a woman's voice on the tempestuous gale. But then there was a flash so vivid that all eyes closed, and the thunder followed with a long and crashing peal.

Marcia groped for her father, threw her arms round his neck, and hid her head on his breast.

" It's the last shot. Look up, silly child. It is over," said he.

She, like a bird who removes its head gradually from under its wing, when the hawk has passed, raised her eyes to his in the gloom, and, still embracing him, said, with a smile which was more in regret than relief :

" I thought we were all killed."

At the same moment, a loud knocking, as with a loaded whipstock, was heard on the outer door through the swish of the clearing-off shower, and a voice, frightened and yet full of self-importance, bellowed :

" Help ! open to my lady ! "

There was the tramp of the servants' feet, a

T

rush of saturated air which blew open the room-door which Mrs. Pleasanton had left ajar, and Keywright, with a lantern, the light extinguished, clattering on his finger by its ring, shouted as he stumbled in :

"Where are you, master ? it's a lady, and her carriage is swamped and smashed by the storm ! "

Two footmen of unusual stature had followed at his heels, and bore, in a long, full mantle of fur, a figure in black travelling costume, so exquisitely shaped that one marvelled at the elements not having respected it, and placing it on its feet, obsequiously supported it. A hood fell back, golden hair streamed, heavy with wet, to the knee, a beautiful face appeared, blue eyes looked piteously out, and, accustomed to the twilight, the lady perceived that she was indoors, safe, unhurt, and that the grey gentleman had risen to receive her.

"This is Colonel Pleasanton," said Keywright, saluting with a wave of the lantern.

Two housemaids, with candles, choked up the doorway, and illumined the now crowded room.

At the name, the lady stepped forward with animation not to have been anticipated, and waving the colonel aside with a small hand accus-tomed to gesture imperiously, stared at Mrs. Pleasanton, who had recoiled from the stranger, and stood behind her husband.

"You are Mrs. Pleasanton, then ? " cried the new-comer. "The woman I seek. I am the

Countess of Fairfield, and I have come to claim my son! Woman, where is my boy?"

Mrs. Pleasanton fell at her feet, uttering in the tone of the prisoner by whom the lot of decimation has been drawn:

"Dead!"

"Dead!" echoed the colonel, who had no eyes or ears for other thing than Marcia, who had sunk back in the chair.

But the lips moved, and, as if he had suddenly been gifted with familiarity with lip-language, he could swear he read in their flutterings:

"Henry not my brother! I may hope!"

CHAPTER XXIX.

A MYRIAD puzzles for the honest, straight-forward soldier were made clear by the denunciation of his wife by the child-hungered mother, for the countess had not feared to reveal (before *servants*, too!) that it was her son, and not her sister's, whom she had been a lifetime seeking. The story of Mrs. Pleasanton on her death-bed, was hardly needed to complete the tale.

Proud of her warlike husband, afraid of his grief at their first child's death turning him for ever from her, she had consented to a scheme of the nurse's suggestion, and substituted Henry for the dead infant. Luckily Pleasanton was out of England. Nevertheless she loathed herself for the deception, and was cold towards the innocent babe. Overhearing her servants comment upon this unnatural behaviour, she changed it diametrically, and was astonished that she felt maternal affection instead of mere pretence. Becoming fond of the boy, for her elder girl, who became Mrs. Pryse-Price, had not touched her heart or removed her fears that the colonel would care little for the wife who had not given him a son, Mrs. Pleasanton was calm enough, till she suspected the real mother might claim her offspring. So, an interminable anxiety, culminating when Mr. Blandford informed her that the woman, in spite of ambition supergratified, had no deeper desire than the recovery of her lost boy. The death of Henry had been but a pause in her punishment. What answer had she when the mother came demanding her child? To fall at her feet, as she had done, for mute entreaty of the impossible pardon.

The colonel stood between her grave and that of the factitious heir.

Fortunately Marcia recovered, and was able to hear that her mother had passed away, without being thrown back.

Elmwood was hateful—graves wherever one turned.

The manager of the Works clamoured for the colonel to return. There were several processes for the products of which heavy contracts had been made, and the colonel from his intimacy with them when he and Rendall had pondered over them in communion, was the only man now to interpret the formulas.

They went back to Gratchley.

They had all the gossip from Mr. Varney; he congratulated them on their return. He had not exactly *planted* yet, but the stakes of demarcation were all set.

"Your daughter and her husband shall plant the first tree," he said.

"You are giving me time to look about, then," she retorted, in her old voice.

Perch was in town; a great seven days' sale was on of the Fairfield Gallery, the old earl being cut up by the illness of his wife, whom Sir John Cutter pronounced incapable of enduring an English winter. He wanted to buy an Italian palace, and take her there.

"They say she is no longer the beauty she was these thirty years—what a long lease an English woman has of loveliness!" sighed Mr. Varney. "The late Mrs. Varney—"

"How is Millward?"

"Hum! shaky! they say the strong fellow in attendance on him is rather a keeper than a valet, and that his knives are silver and his food is served cut."

"And his daughters?"

"Miss Millward is in his yacht. The other at home. There is a dark-faced gentleman, stout and thick-lipped, often there."

"Mr. Goddard?"

"That's it. They'll make a match of it. Sorry to see your daughter so thin—but I'll send you over some of my port, finest in the county"

The colonel settled down in harness, as a

regimental charger turned out to grass after a wound, takes his place on recovery. White where he had been grey, asking a question to be repeated now and then, complaining that the smoke of the chimney prevented him seeing the time by Overdene church clock, still men thought him much the same. At every step he missed Carroll, and when a man would refer to him as an authority of how something was done " in the old days," the colonel would back him up promptly, and " remember " him on pay-day, as he stood by the cashier at his divided trays of gold, silver and bronze.

He met with the name of Wightwarden in the German scientific journals, but it had not the familiar aspect of his chemist's, and he gave up reading the text that tried his eyes.

One day the Works were in jubilee. A process had yielded far beyond expectations, which was all the more gratifying as a delegation of the great company concerned, foreigners glittering with medals, had paid Mr. Pleasanton a visit. They were all in the manager's office, drinking champagne, when a series of low explosions were heard, not enough to alarm anybody ; but suddenly there were shouts, the bell rang, the whistle blew,—when they stepped out a sheet of flame rose like a screen half across the great interior, noiselessly, which added to the horror. Then groans arose behind it ; men, stupefied, were aroused by the pain of burning alive.

" Take my daughter away ; get these gentlemen out of the reach of explosion, they are my guests ; save my guests, men ! " cried the colonel, taking command without hesitation. " Remember those carboys of picratic liquor, Varnardo. Here, a dozen of you, three double pairs, follow me. Men without families ! Come along, boys ! Not you, Jem, you have three children ! Come ! "

At the head of his squad he plunged through the screen of flame. They failed to reappear. No sound, no sight of them. It was horrible anguish to look and listen ; while still the flame, orange and blue, flared smoothly aloft, without much smoke.

The bravest workmen, accustomed to move among acids that would bare a horse's bones with one gallon, powders of which one ounce would bring the thickest wall on a level with its lowest layer of stones—even these recoiled towards the doorway.

Suddenly one of the gentlemen, who had been peculiarly modest among the princes of science and capital, discarding the pale-blue spectacles which had veiled his eyes, sprang forward, no longer with a German accent.

" Stander, Jem, Corker ! lend me a hand ! " he cried.

The three men started and grinned. It was Carroll, who had joined the delegation, nameless on the list, to see his former employer without being known.

The four bounded across a chaos of sand moulds, blackened beams, smoking piles of dampened cinders, with a success born of familiarity, and seizing each an axe, a club, an iron bar, or some handy implement, struck, all as one man, at the corner support of an iron tank. At the fifth blow the leg was broken and the tank tilted over towards them, They leaped aside ; a milky fluid rushed upon the ground where the flame was advancing, and spreading wide and towards it, a subdued hissing was heard. Hercules had strangled the serpent. The fire was extinguished as if a giant foot stamped it out. The screen of flame had vanished like a mirage. Then all saw the men who had been missed, and the saving party, sunk in attitudes of stupor, like the inhabitants of the Castle of the Sleeping Beauty.

The medical men sprang forward : men who wore diamond rings for the restoration of imperial lives, and resuscitated the poisoned workmen. Marcia and the ladies of the neighbourhood vied with the sufferers' wives in attention to the grimy fellows.

Thanks to Carroll's adoption of the most power-ful agent there to quell the substance in flame, against which water and force would have been equally ineffectual, not a man lost his life. The worst affected was the colonel, who had reached the thick of the vapour and snatched up a body, when he was overpowered.

Nevertheless the doctor said he would recover; question of time. Of nursing there was none, for Marcia was only too thankful to repay her father in kind for his devotion during her convalescence.

" He is progressing finely," said Carroll, as he sat with Marcia in their old place by the piano, where they had danced the puppet on the wires, and gummed the letters on the keys, to make papa learn more easily. " I do not say that he will be romping with you next spring; but he can go by slow stages to that Venice where you used to say you longed to dwell."

The heat was suffocating. The windows were open, and the lamp attracted moths, which flitted like early snowflakes. As the daylight gradually disappeared, the words and thoughts of the lovers melted into that quiet, dreamy contemplation to which twilight is so favourable. Soon all conversation ceased beneath the calm beauty of evening. Carroll held the girl's hand, pressing it from time to time. The night fell. The whole room became obscure. Marcia closed her eyes, bent upwards, and her lips appeared to be murmuring a prayer. Then, with an expression of matchless happiness, which surprised even her lover, she said,—

" Oh! how happy I am again to have you by me, my own brave boy! We two shall have a long laugh at those who prophesied a lonely life for the Tomboy!"

"Hark!" cried Wightwarden, starting up. "Who is in your father's room? That sounds like a man's step; he was not able to get up without my arm!"

"Run and see!"

The young gentleman forced a laugh,

"It is nothing! but anyway, I'll take the short cut which I beat you in—in those Tomboy days."

He leaped out of the window, used the trellis of the verandah for a ladder, and so reaching the roof bounded in at the window of the colonel's room, long before the girl had reached even the foot of the stairs within. To his unutterable amazement, the old man, nailed to his couch as he thought, had risen, left the bed, draped in the counterpane like the personification of France enfolded in the tricolour, and, on the apparition of the intruder, smiled, stared at him vacantly from hollowed eyes, saying faintly but triumphantly :—

"Come in, sir! Rescued a comrade and saved the colours!"

In his confused mind, the saving of the workman at the Works was classed with his deeds on the battlefields.

Carroll had barely the time to catch him, replace him on the bed, and rush to the door, which he opened only a little.

"You cannot come in, Marcia. Send for Dr. Davis—quick!"

She descended the stairs, comprehending the event. He turned to the father of his sweetheart, but the old soldier was cold as his sword, which still trembled on the wall from the shock of the young man's alighting in the room.

CHAPTER XXX.

MARCIA'S dream was realised, and like all dreams when solidified, shrunk into moderate dimensions. Nevertheless she liked Venice, and was never tired of studying the details after she and her husband had mastered the general effect. One day their landlord, of the Magnifico, came to them "in desolation of heart."

"Only for t'ree day," he implored. "You oblige me for t'ree leetle day—to give up your suite—I make you ze comfort like a royal couple in the other wing; but it is an ancient patron, milordo Fairfield; and you being of the English, know how they like the same old apartments."

"We are going out in a sailing-boat for a couple of days, you can have the rooms," replied Wightwarden. "Keywright, just see our own little traps are shifted properly."

However, they did not quite succeed avoiding the rencontre with the bearer of a name which recalled the dolorous night of Marcia's worst memories.

On the stairs they saw descending, upon their return from the water promenade, a sort of procession such as foreign hotel proprietors love to arrange for exceptional guests. A vanguard of servants, four English footmen, two by two, with my lady's and my lord's carriage wraps, a gentleman in black, with a chain like a segment of an ocean cable.

" The steward of milord," whispered the servants at the back of Mr. Wightwarden and his wife; and in a lower tone, " Cicisbeo."

" Blandford ! " thought the Englishman.

Then a very old man, bowed, trembling, on the arm of a woman, fair, tall, majestic ; not so much English as one of those Venetians who wore pattens to exalt themselves physically, even as they had raised themselves above the herd by their insuperable pride.

Marcia drew her husband back ; but the insolent dame did not favour the bystanders with a glance.

" Cicely ! " she murmured.

In vain had Mr. Millward, while in his senses, planned to punish his daughter for her unfilial greed by cutting her off. She had secured the prize dropped from the dead hand of the ignoble beauty, despoiling her of her jewels, title and wealth, with less remorse than Mrs. Pleasanton had robbed her of the child of her poverty.

The outcry was overheard. The arrogant head

turned, and the eyes of Cicely met for the final time those of our hero.   Hers were cold, lifeless, inhuman; that poor octogenarian was the vulture's prey.   His were glowing, overflowing with warmth and bliss.   Countess though she was, her heart grew cold with envy at Marcia's happier fate.

THE END.

WILLIAM RIDER AND SON, PRINTERS, LONDON.

www.ingramcontent.com/pod-product-compliance
Lightning Source LLC
Chambersburg PA
CBHW021044030726
47496CB00006B/1687